Enigma Winds

- A Novel -

Marilynn J. Harris

Cottage Publishing

Cottage Publishing
Boise, Idaho
www.marilynnjharris.com

First published by Cottage Publishing 4/4/2014

ISBN-13: 978-0692026854 (Cottage Publishing)

ISBN-10: 0692026851

Printed in the United States of America

For information or to order more books please visit our website:
www.marilynnjharris.com

Or Contact:
Cottage Publishing
8530 W Targee Street
Boise, ID 83709

Also by Marilynn J. Harris

The Moon Mountain Series

On Top of Moon Mountain: book one

Beyond The Idaho Mountains: book two

Return To Terror Mountain: book three

The Enigma Series

Enigma Fire: book one

With loving appreciation to my sister
and my proficient husband

"The Wind beneath My Wings"

TABLE OF CONTENTS

ONE	What I Remember	1
TWO	On The Road Again	4
THREE	Bad Dreams	18
FOUR	Sleep	22
FIVE	Unexplainable	28
SIX	Football You Bet	31
SEVEN	Life Goes On	34
EIGHT	Read On	41
NINE	As The World Turns	48
TEN	We Love Our Grandkids	53
ELEVEN	The Winds	59
TWELVE	Idaho History	66
THIRTEEN	Safe-Haven	72
FOURTEEN	Tower County	86
FIFTEEN	The Cavern	99
SIXTEEN	The Conference	116
SEVENTEEN	The Honeybee	127
EIGHTEEN	Disaster	140
NINETEEN	The Chopper	151
TWENTY	The Beekeepers	157
TWENTY-ONE	The Entomologist	162
TWENTY-TWO	The Answer	171
TWENTY-THREE	An Act Of God	178
TWENTY-FOUR	The Dead Bees	183
TWENTY-FIVE	Crisis	194
TWENTY-SIX	Our Friends Arrive	203
TWENTY-SEVEN	The Community	210
TWENTY-EIGHT	Home Sweet Home	216

ONE

What I Remember

It was early October and several months had passed since my accident in Garden Valley. Yet still I remembered nothing of the actual incident. Many people had tried to jog my memory by sharing their recollection of that horrible night. Friends had described to me in detail the events of the accident. They had recounted every possible aspect of the evening hoping in some way to help me remember, but what I remembered was not at all as they described.

I do remember some things about that evening. I remember packing for our trip to Florida that we were taking with our kids the following day. I knew that I had everything organized and waiting at the front door so that we would be ready to go on Wednesday morning.

I also remember meeting the Tuesday night motorcycle group for the dinner ride up to Garden Valley.

We had a large group of riders that evening and I vaguely recall the ride up the canyon to the restaurant.

When we were at the restaurant we were all sitting in one long table out on the covered patio. Our group always sat at that same table every time we ate dinner in Garden Valley. Everyone talked and laughed and shared their plans for the summer; and I faintly remember Tom standing up to go find the waitress.

But what I remember most about that evening was all of the blackbirds. I can still see the multitudes of blackbirds as they shot up towards the sky from every direction. For some reason that is where my recollection of that Tuesday evening begins to blur. From that point on my mind recalls a completely different series of events. Nothing I remember is at all like what has been told to me by the people that were there that evening.

For the first few weeks after I regained consciousness the bizarre thoughts in my troubled brain began to fade. I had persuaded myself that everything that I thought had happened while I was unconscious was mere complications caused by my severe head injury. I constantly persuaded my mind to move forward so that I could get on with living. I continually argued with myself trying to inform my emotions that none of the events really happened. As the days passed by I refused to even think about the weird happenings that had been consuming my mind.

Even after I had read the events from the old newspapers stating that most of the things that I remembered had actually happened on those dates; I was forced to dismiss any similarities. I knew that I couldn't have really been there. I had been in the hospital in a coma at the time the events were taking place. I was unconscious and there is no possible way that any of the things that I recalled during those weeks could have been real. Yet the newspaper confirmed the dates, the towns and the horror that I thought my Christian Motorcyclists Association friends and I had been through.

Every day I tried desperately to move on with my life and to ignore any of the nightmares that I believed were real. No matter how frightened I sometimes became, I never once shared my fears or thoughts with anyone else. I was sure that they would think that I was crazy and delusional because of the accident, so I confided in no one.

TWO

On The Road Again

Six weeks after I regained consciousness I was released from the doctor. I was beginning to feel like a regular person again. I had no pain and I was able to take short walks each day as I regained my strength. I was so happy to be getting back to a normal life.

The weather in Boise was unusually warm for the month of October. It was perfect conditions for a late fall motorcycle ride up to the mountains, but we knew the weather could change any day. The daytime temperatures were hovering around 71 degrees and the evenings temperatures were only dropping to the low 50's.

The doctor had released me so that I could start riding the motorcycle again. I was more than ready to get back on our Gold Wing

Trike for a quick dinner ride up to Idaho City with our friends from CMA (Christian Motorcyclists Association). Although I had often visited with many of the members since I had regained consciousness this was the first time that my husband and I had actually ridden with all of them as a group since before the accident.

It was so invigorating to move on and forget the terrifying images that had been trapped inside of my subconscious mind. I had been constantly trying to trick myself into believing that everything was back to the way it was before the mishap. I almost had myself convinced, but then something unusual happened when we met with the group that day that caused my mind to once again slip back into the deep confusion that I had been fighting so hard to overcome.

Our group always met at a central parking lot before going on a ride. After visiting with everyone for a few minutes and praying together for a safe ride up to the mountains it was time for us to get on our motorcycles and head up to Idaho City.

Just as I was walking to our trike to get ready to go my friend Terrell motioned for me to come over by their bike. She said, "I have something for you in the trunk of our motorcycle."

When I walked over to her trunk she handed me our giant battery lantern. I began to violently shake because I knew I had never loaned her the lantern. I cautiously ask her, "But where did you get this?" She didn't answer me she just smiled and turned around and climbed on the back of their trike to get ready to leave.

My hands were trembling so viciously that I could hardly control them as I moved my purse around in the trunk to make room for the lantern so that we could go. I put the lid down on the trunk and when I climbed into place on the back of the trike I could barely think. My husband never even questioned me about the lantern. I'm sure he assumed that I had loaned it to Terrell and Eddie some time ago and they were just now giving it back to me.

Seeing the giant battery lantern again caused my thoughts to ignite. Every fear that I had overcome in the past several weeks rapidly returned. My mind was once again disorientated. I was horrified; my entire being was overwhelmed with panic.

As we traveled up highway 21 towards Idaho City I never once noticed the beautiful fall colors or the shallow flowing Mores Creek as we meandered along the peaceful mountain highway. My husband mentioned several menial things to me through the headset, but I didn't talk, I couldn't talk because my mind was completely inundated. My entire being was utterly overwhelmed, I felt weak all over because I knew where Terrell had gotten the lantern, but it just couldn't be.

I was in the hospital at the time she got the lantern, I was unconscious. I was in a coma. The events that I thought I had lived through were not true. Yet I knew how she had gotten the lantern; I had given it to her.

She had put the lantern in her trailer when we were packing up to leave at the old abandoned farmhouse where we had spent the night on our journey through the darkness. It was on the nineteenth day of our travels and we were heading up towards Chicago trying to get around the raging fire storm that had consumed so much of the area.

She had taken the lantern to store it for me. As we were packing the trailers and getting ready to leave the farmhouse that day, I started laughing because my trailer was just too crowded. I would move one thing around and then replace it with something else. We were trying to get the trailers packed up so that after we went up on the roof with the telescope we would be all ready to go.

Our trailer was stuffed because of all the bulky new clothes that we had purchased. My husband Darrell and I carried the telescope and a lot of the food and cooking materials in our trailer, so we were already overloaded.

Every one of us had gotten new clothes at a large department store in Kansas a few days earlier. We had been forced to find heavier clothing because each day as we traveled towards the light the weather got colder and colder because there was no sunlight. The temperature seemed to be dropping about two degrees each day and the clothing we had originally packed had to be thrown away and replaced with bulkier items. I had been over-cramming everything inside our trailer for the past several days.

When Terrell saw me trying to load the crowded trailer that day she offered to carry some of my stuff in her trailer. That is when she had taken the large lantern from me and placed it in her trailer because she had more room than I did.

The lantern was unique I had never seen another one like it before. It was twice the size of any of the other battery-type lanterns that you could buy at a department store. I had special ordered it for my husband Darrell's birthday a year earlier, so when Terrell gave it back to me there was no mistake that it was the same giant lantern that I had given her at the farmhouse.

My mind started to whirl as I remembered in vivid detail the old abandoned farmhouse that we had stayed in. We had not seen any other houses, barns or out-buildings for miles. We were so grateful to have found the old house and to have some place to spend the night, just to get out of the cold.

Our group had to sleep on the floor in sleeping bags in the large front room, but we didn't care because we had been traveling for hours and we were utterly worn out. We were just thankful to have a place to get inside because we were cold and extremely exhausted from traveling all day.

It wasn't until the next morning that we discovered the atrocity in the upstairs attic. Darrell led the group up the dark stairs looking for a place to set up the telescope so we could get our bearings to head towards the light. Setting up the telescope and searching for daylight was a ritual that we went through every single day.

We walked in unison up the dark stairway trying to get to the roof of the old farmhouse; stumbling over each other and giggling because we were walking so close together. It was very dark and eerie inside the narrow stairway, but I vividly remember all of us creeping up the pitch-black stairs trying to reach the attic.

As I sat there frantically quivering on the back of the motorcycle my whole being was besieged with the remembrance of that day. I again felt like vomiting as I brought to mind the horrendous smell coming from the attic as we approached the top of the stairs. The door to the attic was locked, but Jim rammed up against it until the old door tore off of its hinges.

Our bright flashlights exposed the shocking evidence left in the attic; we could see large masses of splattered blood that covered the walls, ceiling and floor. People had obviously been killed there. The old abandoned farmhouse had been used as some sort of torture chamber.

The house was out in the middle of nowhere and it would have been the perfect location for someone to use for a house of horrors because there was no one else around for miles. The entire room was completely enclosed; there was no way to escape. Even the small windows were securely nailed shut making the disturbing attic an enclosed tomb.

We innocently spent the night in that hideous place. We had slept right down stairs in the front room unaware of the revulsion that had once taken place in the attic. I shook my head and closed my eyes to erase the horrible images that I could see inside of my brain, but they wouldn't go away because the images were too real.

I wanted to cover my face and crawl into a corner and hide, but as I put my hands to my face I realized my motorcycle helmet was in the way. My thoughts were forced back to reality. I had to remind myself that everything was all right and that I was on the back of the trike on my way up to Idaho City to have dinner with our friends. Once again I convinced my brain that everything was back to normal, and I had nothing to fear because none of these things that I remembered were real.

But I felt absolutely drained; maybe I really wasn't strong enough to get out on the motorcycle this soon. I thought my mind was back to thinking straight, but I again felt thoroughly confused. For weeks I had been forced to accept the fact that I had been unconscious after my accident and that none of the horrible events that I remembered could have really happened.

Yet I had read about the gruesome abandoned farmhouse in the newspaper while I was recovering. When I read about it I knew exactly where it was located, because I had been there. If none of this really happened, how did Terrell get the lantern? I felt very mixed up; nothing made any sense at all.

When we finally reached the restaurant at Idaho City I got off of the trike and decided I would take my friend Terrell aside and tell her about the weird things that had been going through my mind since my accident. She must know something because she had my lantern and Terrell might be the only person who would understand.

I took a deep breathe and started over to talk with her: it was time to tell someone about my puzzling thoughts. Perhaps Terrell could shed some light on all of my confusion since she had been with us in Garden Valley when I had the accident. Just knowing where she got the lantern would help me get some of my questions answered. Maybe I did loan it to her and I just can't remember.

As I approached her she was busy visiting with Bobbi about something. They were having a very serious conversation and then they both burst out laughing and started walking towards the restaurant. They were really wrapped up in their conversation so I hated to interrupt them.

As I watched them walk away I decided this was not the right time to ask her about the lantern. I would just wait until a more convenient time when we were all alone. As I studied her walking towards the restaurant I could tell that giving me back my lantern was not a big deal to her. She acted calm and carefree and yet I felt so serious and anxious about everything. My insides were quivering because obviously I was the only one concerned about how she had gotten the lantern in the first place.

"How would I even approach her about the subject?" I thought to myself. "What would I say to her?" She didn't act upset or concerned she acted like she had just given me back my lantern after she borrowed it and there was nothing more to say, but that confused me even more. I didn't want to talk to her about it in front of anyone else so I decided to just forget about it for now and bring it up at another time when we could talk alone.

When we got inside the restaurant Terrell and her husband Eddie sat at the opposite end of the table so we couldn't really talk with them. Tom and Margaret were sitting directly across from us while Darlene and her husband Jerry sat on our left side, and Tom and Bobbi were sitting on the right.

As I watched Terrell during dinner she honestly didn't seem concerned about anything. She casually smiled at me once in awhile and then just continued to visit with everyone around her. I told myself to breathe and relax and to forget about how she got the lantern.

Everyone in our group seemed so relaxed that I knew there had to be a logical explanation for everything that had gone on. We were all very comfortable as a group because we ate dinner together every Tuesday night. Each one of us looked forward to getting together every week and just having a peaceful dinner with good friends.

I glanced down the table and studied each one of my friends carefully; they all seemed to be having a good time and I could tell by watching them that I was the only one that was frazzled about anything.

As I stopped and carefully listened to them talk I realized that they were innocently talking about football. The Boise State Broncos had won every game again this year and as each person talked they got more and more excited. They described each game play by play as if no one else had really seen it. As they talked their voices got louder with each comment and I couldn't help but get caught up in their enthusiasm. Our family loved football and we lived for the football season.

Our second grandson was playing on the Cole Valley Christian team this year. It was his senior year and they too had won every game. It was an exciting year for the team because it was the first time in the school's history that they were unbeaten.

Just thinking about football made me feel better. "Maybe I am just confused because of my accident," I thought to myself. "No one else seems concerned about anything; they were all laughing and talking and enjoying their dinner. So, that is what I need to do too. I must just accept the fact that everything is back to normal and move on."

After we ate dinner we gorged ourselves on Trudy's famous homemade pie. Darrell and I shared a piece of coconut cream and it was delicious, but I was feeling weary. Trying to act healthy and pretending that everything is okay is very exhausting. Even after resting for the past several weeks I was ready to go back to bed. I hadn't been out of the house much since my accident and I decided I still needed more rest. I knew that I would see things a lot clearer once I got caught up on my sleep and I truly would feel stronger.

We finished dinner and everyone sat around the table and visited and as we talked I began to calm down. I slowly forgot about the lantern. I began talking and joining in on the conversations with everyone. We had moved on from football to telling cute stories about our grandkids. And of course my grandkids were my favorite subject and my husband and I had many clever things to share that our grandchildren had said and done.

I was laughing and totally enjoying myself when Darlene decided to take off her leather jacket. After sitting in the restaurant for awhile we were all feeling a lot warmer. Several people had already removed their heavy jackets, but it wasn't until Darlene took off her jacket that I noticed the beautiful sweater that she was wearing under her coat. I stared at her in disbelief and once again I couldn't think straight.

"I remember when she got that sweater," I said to myself. "We were all together at a large department store in Kansas when we were on our journey through the darkness."

Margaret, Bobbi and Darlene and I had bought sweaters alike. We were so cold all of the time and we needed something to keep us warm.

The sweaters were very bulky, but they were really soft so we each got two in different colors.

The weather was getting colder every day and we were forced to find heavier clothes to wear. Without the sunlight we just couldn't keep warm enough. We were excited when we found the sweaters in a back room at a huge department store because it was off-season and it was Kansas, so we were lucky to find sweaters at all.

Margaret chose a tan one and a burgundy color, I got a beautiful red one and a black one, Bobbi got a brown one and a white one and of course Darlene picked out a black sweater and the gorgeous green one that she was now wearing.

My insides were again shaking and I was almost afraid to ask, but I timidly commented to Darlene, "What a beautiful green sweater. Where did you get it?"

"Thank you don't you just love the color?" Darlene gloated, "I got it when we were on a trip a few weeks ago. I don't remember exactly where, but I sure do like it. It is really warm and it is so soft." Then she casually just turned away and started telling her husband Jerry something.

No one else commented on her new sweater or even acted interested at all. Bobbi was right next to her and she just glanced at Darlene and went right on talking about something else. If Bobbi really did have a matching brown and a white sweater like Darlene's she didn't mention it.

"Am I losing my mind?" I questioned inside of my head. Again my thoughts began to race. "Where did Darlene get that green sweater? Everything is getting confused again," I contemplated as I buried my face into my hands. I closed my eyes and sat quietly and just listened to the chattering voices talking all around me. My friends were all talking, but I feared that I was going to scream. I wanted to get up from the table and just disappear. They were innocently talking and laughing, but I was absolutely climbing out of my skin and I could think of nothing else to talk to anyone about.

Darlene noticed that I was having a hard time because I had my head down and I had my face buried in my hands. She surprised me when she put her hand on my shoulder. "Are you all right?" She asked in a very concerned voice.

She startled me when she touched my shoulder with the sleeve of her green sweater. It was as if a lightening bolt jumped from her arm to my shoulder pulsating through the mysterious green sweater and entering into my back and neck. It felt like a strong shock of electricity mysteriously passing between us as she caringly touched my shoulder. We both jumped and squealed at the same time as the questionable sweater sent painful jolts through both of our bodies.

"What just happened?" Darlene shouted as she rubbed her arm and instantly pulled her hand away from my shoulder.

"I'm not sure," I commented as I moved my shoulders and neck back and forth. "For some reason your sweater sent shock waves through both of us."

The shock waves were so violent that everyone up and down the table could see them. Everybody was murmuring and commenting about the massive blue sparks that had jumped from Darlene's sweater to my shoulders.

"Oh, I am so sorry," Darlene sincerely apologized still rubbing her aching arm. "Are you all right? I can't believe the strength of the shock waves that it sent. That really hurt. You have been through so much in the past few months I hope that you are okay."

I smiled as I continued to stretch my neck and rub my shoulders. "Oh I'll be fine," I said trying to convince her that it wasn't a big deal. Yet, I knew something strange had just happened. It was as if the sweater recognized me just as I had recognized it.

I had never experienced anything so weird in my life. I knew that I wasn't dreaming or unconscious this time. I was wide awake and what had just happened was real. Everyone at the table saw it. They could see the sparks as they leaped violently through the air.

My entire body ached and I was overly exhausted. All I could think about was going home and going to bed. I knew I would feel better once I rested for awhile and I could clear my thoughts. Surely I would come up with a reasonable explanation for everything that was going on and the recent upsetting events would make more sense once I slept for a few days and stayed away from everyone.

I decided that if I didn't talk to anyone or see anyone for awhile I could sort out some of the puzzling things that were rambling around inside my head. Obviously I was the only one that knew anything about our travels through the darkness so they could not be real, but something uncanny was going on.

Perhaps the day of the darkness was something that I created in my own mind while I was in a coma. But then there was the battery lantern and now the shock waves through the sweater. I had no idea what was happening, but I felt sure that if I slept for a few days and cleared my thoughts I would be able to understand a lot better about what was going on. There had to be a rational explanation for everything. Maybe I could figure things out once I got a lot of sleep and could be alone with my thoughts.

I had to get a grip on my situation or I would soon drive myself crazy with all of my absurd ideas. I was so relieved when everyone finished dinner and it was time to go back to Boise. I practically ran out to the trike to leave. I didn't want to talk to anyone else. I just wanted to get home and hide.

When I got on the trike to head back towards town I closed my eyes and I prayed. I was so confused and afraid and I needed strength to cope with all of the unexplainable things that were going on. I felt so disorientated about everything and it seemed like my whole world was out of control. I ask the Lord for wisdom and peace. I could not understand why I felt so extremely mixed up and everyone around me seemed so unaffected.

We had traveled all of the way down the mountain on highway 21 before I finally started to think clearer. We passed Hill Top and were on our way around Lucky Peak Dam headed for Diversion Dam when I suddenly realized what I needed to do. I knew that I couldn't talk to anyone about my feelings or my confused ideas. This was something I needed to figure out on my own. I would not be able to confide my wild thoughts in any other person. I knew that no one would understand. I could tell by the way everyone had reacted at dinner that they were completely unaware of any of the events that I felt had taken place during the past several months.

I knew that all of their lives were still the same. Only mine had gone through some kind of disruption, some kind of peculiar change. Perhaps it was the head injury that had occurred during the accident. All I knew for certain was that I needed to rest for the next several days to try to clear my head. After that I was sure that I would be able to think straighter and then I could face whatever was ahead of me. Hopefully I would be able to find answers to my confusion.

For now sleep was the answer. I was positive that after I caught up on my rest I would be able to sort out what was real and what was not real.

THREE

Bad Dreams

I thought we would never get back home from Idaho City. I was so tired I could hardly stay awake on the back of the bike. I was ready to go straight to bed. My mind was going in circles and my thoughts could not calm down. Too many things just didn't add up. All I wanted to do was go to sleep and forget the strange events of the evening. It was nice seeing all of my friends again, but after getting the lantern back and seeing Darlene in her green sweater I felt more confused than I did before.

I took a quick bath and climbed into bed around 10:15. I instantly fell into a deep heavy sleep, but I had only slept for about 2 hours when I awoke in a cold sweat. I looked at the clock and I could see that I had only been asleep for a short while. It was 12:22 in the morning.

For several minutes I lay quietly in our dark bedroom unable to move. I was overcome by the enormous fear that my world would once again be encompassed in total darkness. Once you live in darkness your existence is never the same. It is so overpowering it is even difficult to breathe. You are absolutely helpless and there is no escape. When you live in total darkness you always carry some sort of light with you wherever you go because your eyes never adjust.

As I lay there in my bedroom with my husband by my side I had to shake my head back and forth to once again clear my thoughts. I had to remind myself that for some reason the day of the darkness was not real. I had not really walked in total darkness. I had not in fact lived in total darkness, but it seemed so true. I could feel it, I could hear the absolute silence, I could see it, and I feared it with all of my being.

I crept out of bed and slowly made my way towards the hall; lightly touching the dresser and walls as I stumbled towards the doorway in the dark. I was trembling as I reached for the light switch in the hallway. I couldn't help myself I was encompassed in fear, too many odd things had happened during the evening to remind me again of that strange time.

I sincerely feared that the day of the darkness was real. I was afraid that when I turned on the switch there would be no light. I felt ill and I could barely move one foot in front of the other because I was so overcome with anxiety.

But as I forced myself to reach for the light switch I exhaled a big sigh of relief because the hall light shown brightly just as it was made to do. It pleasantly lit up the entire hallway and I almost cried out loud. "I can see," I felt like screaming to the top of my lungs. "The darkness did not return."

As I slowly crept down the hallway to the front room I walked around and turned on every lamp and light fixture just as I had done so many times before. Overcoming the darkness was my immediate challenge and once again I had won.

I carefully sat down on the couch up next to a table lamp and turned the switch to the highest beam. I glanced up at the dining room clock glowing brightly above the dinning room table. It was now 12:36 and I had been awake for fifteen minutes.

After sitting there silently for a few seconds I realized that the clock in the bedroom had also been working or I wouldn't have been able to tell what time it was when I first woke up. In my bewildered state of mind I didn't understand that right away. If the darkness had returned the electricity wouldn't have been working. I had been in such a deep sleep when I woke up and our bedroom was so dark that it confused me and I couldn't think straight.

For a second I felt embarrassed by my confusion until I realized that no one else even knew that I was mixed up and that I was afraid that the power was gone again. All of my feelings were once more hidden safely inside of my head, but I felt so unsettled. I had a hard time keeping my thoughts straight in my mind. My brain was on overload, and the events of the evening had once again befuddled my thinking and I was finding it hard to distinguish reality from make-believe.

I sat there quietly for several hours trying to sort things out. I was silently waiting for the light of dawn so that I could relax. When the sun finally came up I put my head back against the couch and closed my eyes to go to sleep. I was so tired, but because I feared the darkness I had patiently waited for the morning sunrise before I dared fall back to sleep.

When my husband woke up he once again walked quietly around the room turning off every light and then he went back to the bedroom to

20

let me sleep. Since my accident my husband had been forced to adjust to the oddities that I oftentimes went through. Several times since I returned from the hospital he had found me sleeping in the front room with every light turned on.

FOUR

Sleep

The days following our ride to Idaho City I remained hidden inside of my house. I didn't want to see anyone. I didn't get dressed or talk to anyone but my husband. I thought that if I stayed away from everyone my confusion would slowly clear up.

I tried and tried, but I could not remember another time that I would have given the battery lantern to Terrell and Eddie. I decided to start taking the sleeping pills that the doctor had given me when I left the hospital. I hadn't taken any of them until now, but I felt that I needed them to get a good night's sleep. I thought that if I slept continually for a few days my mind would be clearer and I could sort out reality from some of my confusing imaginings.

Within a few days I really did feel better. I felt fully rested, but I still had no answers to the perplexing questions about the lantern and the sweater. I could no longer trick my brain into ignoring the events that I felt sure had really happened. When I was awake I would sit for hours trying to categorize everything that people had told me about the accident in Garden Valley, but nothing really made any sense to me.

I had slept for almost an entire week when I finally felt well enough to get up and get dressed. I was so much better it was like I was a new person. My mind was clear and I no longer felt anxious. I was ready to face whatever was ahead. I still had no answers to my confusion, but I knew after several days of sleeping that I was strong enough to handle my strange situation.

My husband Darrell was so glad to have me up and feeling better that he convinced me to get out of the house for awhile and go for a ride in the car. It felt so relaxing just to drive around and forget all of the baffling things that had been going on in my mind.

While I'd been sleeping the weather had gotten considerably cooler and the leaves were turning various shades of gold, red and auburn. Many of the streets were covered with the fallen leaves. It was a beautiful time of year to get out and enjoy the wonderful colors of autumn. Going for a ride was a great idea.

After driving around for nearly two hours we stopped at the Big Bun Drive-In on Overland and bought hamburgers, tater tots and cokes. They always gave us more tater tots than even three people could eat so we wrapped the leftovers up in a napkin to take home for later. The food tasted wonderful.

It was amazing just getting out of the house again for a few hours. I was glad that my husband had suggested it. I had forgotten all about the lantern and the sweater. They no longer consumed all of my thoughts.

23

Since I had caught up on my sleep I felt so much better that I decided it was time for me to get out into the world again. I had not driven the car or been anywhere by myself since my accident in June. I planned to go to at least one place every day. I would go shopping or to the store or go and visit a friend. I knew that getting out of the house was the only way that I was going to pull myself out of the nightmare that I had been living in.

I had convinced my mind that the strange things about the lantern and Darlene's sweater were of no importance any longer. It was time to just accept things as they were and to move on. I may never have any answers or solutions to my questions, but I decided that whatever happens I will be all right. I was rested, I was getting healthier every day and I knew that soon everything in my life would be settled.

Our grandson had a football game this evening and I was going to surprise my husband and go with him. This week's game will be much colder than the last game that I went to so I will have to bundle up, but no matter how cold it is... I am going. "If anything can get my thinking back to the way that it was, it would be football," I thought with a smile.

I am sure that my husband would not expect me to go with him tonight, because I had been sleeping all week and I hadn't gone anywhere else until today. But, I am an avid football fan and I get totally wrapped up in the game and going to the game should be good therapy.

As we pulled into the driveway I had completely forgotten about my accident because my head felt clearer than it had for along time. It was as if an enormous burden had been taken off of my shoulders and I was ready to get on with my life and I could face anything that I needed to face.

We went to the mailbox and got the mail and then we headed for our front door. I was shuffling through some cards and letters and as I was sorting over the rest of the mail I looked up and discovered that my husband had found something on the deck. I was surprised to see him holding an old coffee pot. He grinned and commented, "Hey what's this?"

Sitting on the front deck table was our old camp coffee pot with a note attached. The note said: I was cleaning out our motorcycle trailer and I discovered your old coffee pot hidden under one of our sleeping bags. Sorry I didn't get it back to you sooner. I have been working on our trailer for two whole days. I spent hours scrubbing it down. I had a terrible time getting the dried salt water off. It was really a mess. I had neglected it for way too long before trying to clean it up and underneath the trailer was solid white powder. The letter was not signed.

Darrell looked at me confused and asked, "Did we loan our old coffee pot to someone? I don't remember."

I just shrugged my shoulders because I really didn't remember either.

"Sounds like whoever we loaned the coffee pot to must have been staying near the Salt Lake area. I can't think of anyplace else that would have gotten their trailer all salty underneath," my husband casually responded as he walked into the house.

I didn't comment. I didn't know what to say, I really didn't know who had brought the coffee pot back to us. All I knew for sure was that we were surrounded by a massive flood by the Great Salt Lake while we were on our journey searching for the light. But my husband had never said anything to me about our trailer having dried salt on it, so I had never even thought about it again.

As Darrell took the coffee pot to the garage to put it away I glanced down at the mail that was still in my hands. There buried under several other letters was a plain white envelope addressed to me. The return address at the top of the envelope said Hartman's Grocery, 4282 West State Street, Evanston, Wyoming.

As I cautiously opened the envelope I immediately recognized the carefully folded yellow paper that we had used on our journey through the darkness. The paper contained a list of all of the groceries that each one of us had collected while we were at the store in Evanston. Each list on the paper was signed by all of the people in our party with everyone's name, phone number and address.

A yellow copy was left at every store to be used as an IOU for payment for all of things that we had purchased from their store. After the day of the darkness occurred we hadn't found any other people anywhere. But we didn't want to just steal whatever we needed as we were traveling so we created the IOU yellow paper system to leave as a means of record keeping.

We couldn't pay for things with money or credit cards like we usually did because there was never anyone to pay. A yellow paper IOU was left at every motel and store to be used as a sign of good-faith. Each of us left all of our information so that if the merchant did return they would know that we were sincere and would have paid them if they had been there and could collect. Leaving an IOU was the only honest way we could think of to acquire the supplies we needed as we traveled towards the light.

Apparently, someone from the store in Evanston had sent me one of the letters that we had left on our journey. I rapidly looked through the envelope and turned it over and over again, but there was nothing else in the envelope, only the yellow paper. There was no explanation of payment due or a signature from the manger or store clerk. I knew what the paper was, but I didn't know what to do with it.

I can't explain it, but for some reason I felt unbelievably calm as I looked over the yellow paper. I didn't feel sick, frightened, disillusioned or distraught like I would have only a few days earlier. The letter should have upset me, but it really didn't. I knew that I must learn to accept things even if they didn't make any sense to me. I realized that this was just the way my world would be from now on and I could not let all of these shocking events confuse my thinking.

When my husband returned from the garage he noticed me holding the yellow paper, but he didn't even comment about it. He just walked on by and headed out to the barn. His reaction seemed so strange to me because this was the type of paper that we had used many times on our trip through the darkness. But I could tell by the way he acted that it did not look familiar to him at all. He never even asked me what it was and I didn't try to hide it from him, but I could tell that he wasn't the least bit curious about the yellow letter.

FIVE

Unexplainable

There are so many things in this world that we cannot explain. Because so many things are absolutely unexplainable: like why are some people healed when they are sick and other people die. Why does Chemotherapy work for some cancer victims and other patients lose the battle?

Why does one child die in a school bus accident when none of the other children are even injured? And then you see a vehicle completely crushed beyond recognition and the driver survives without a scratch.

How does a person live through 10 hours of surgery only to die two months later of a heart attack?

Why do some unhealthy people live to be a hundred and a long distance marathon runner dies of a heart attack at 44 years old?

One of my sorority sisters watched out the hospital window as a severe lightening storm lit up the entire sky. As her husband lay in a hospital bed dying of cancer she turned to him with tears in her eyes and said, "Jesus has come for you dear." And her husband squeezed her hand and smiled at her; then he closed his eyes and died.

So many people believe in angels even though they cannot see them, they know that they are always there.

How do some Christians die and go to heaven and then come back to life to tell others about the light?

Why do many mothers wake up in the middle of the night and have a strong fear that something is wrong with someone that they love; only to find out that their fears were correct?

How does a two hundred year old Oak tree survive through a massive hurricane and still continue to hold on tightly to its leaves? When the storm stops and everything around the tree is completely destroyed the tree stands proud and firm as if nothing unusual had happened.

Why do some people say goodbye and give an extra hug as if they know that it will be their final goodbye?

How does a premature baby with no chance of survival grow into a healthy normal adult?

My friend lost her husband a few years ago and on the way to his funeral the dome light in her car lit up. She hysterically bowed her head over the steering wheel and cried out to her husband, "What am I supposed to do? You always fixed everything." And the light went off.

There are so many questions in this world that cannot be answered. So maybe my thoughts of the events of the darkness are not so hard to believe.

There are even questions about things that I do myself that I have often wondered about: like why do I automatically wake up every morning at 5:14...sixteen minutes before the alarm is set to ring? No matter where I am or what time I go to bed I will always wake up several minutes before the alarm goes off; even if it is set for 3:00 or 4:00 in the morning. The uncanny thing is I have only heard the alarm go off a few times in my entire lifetime. Every morning I wake up and turn it off ahead of time. I set it every night, but I rarely need it.

I may never know what happened to me in Garden Valley or why my world has been so completely changed, but I know that I must learn to adjust to whatever my new life brings. I feel so lucky because whatever else has changed since my accident, I still have my husband, my health and my loving family.

I was telling my husband the truth about the coffee pot, I really don't know who had brought it back to us and left it on the deck. But I do know that we had used that same coffee pot every single day when we were traveling with our friends. I also remember that all of our trailers were covered in dried salt water after we escaped the flooding near Salt Lake City when we were on our long journey.

For the first time in weeks I felt completely at peace. I felt no panic, but I knew that I must be careful what I mention to anyone from now on.

SIX

Football You Bet

I was so excited to get dressed to go to the football game that evening. Tonight it is football for Cole Valley Christian and tomorrow night it is the Boise State Broncos. Watching football is the perfect medicine to get my life back on track.

I put on two pairs of socks and a set of Under Armor, then my Levi's. As I was searching through my dresser for something warm to wear I came across my new bulky black sweater that I had purchased in Kansas, the one that matched Darlene's sweater. I quickly put it on and smiled as I looked at myself in the mirror. The beautiful black sweater was really soft and extremely warm. It would be perfect for the icy-cold weather that had seemed to come in overnight. The temperature had been dropping several degrees every evening since we got back from Idaho

City. Idaho's weather is like that it can change 30 degrees in two days and with the wind chill it could seem much colder than that.

I usually wear the Cole Valley Christian colors to the football games, but tonight it is so cold I will need to wear a heavy coat over my clothes anyway. Even if I wore a Cole Valley shirt no one would be able to see it.

The game was even colder than we expected, it was absolutely freezing, but we didn't care because once again the Cole Valley Chargers came out ahead. Their team was unbelievable this year. What a great way for our grandson to end his senior year, never losing a game. You couldn't help but get caught up in all of the excitement of the fans. We thoroughly enjoyed sitting with all of the parents, grandparents and their families. It was the greatest football season the school had ever had and we loved being a part of it.

After the game we went to Red Robin with our kids to meet up with the team and their families. This was a special memory that we would remember for the rest of our lives. We were so blessed to always be included. The team and their families met at Red Robin after every home game.

I was very exhausted after a long day of staying awake, but I felt so much better. My thoughts were clearer, I had gone out for a drive and to lunch with my husband, and then to the game and to Red Robin with the group. I was ready for a good night's rest.

After a hot bath I was out like a light. As I slept I once again dreamed of my travels through the darkness, but this time they were comforting thoughts not frightening dreams like I had dreamed before. I was no longer trying to forget our journey through the darkness. I was ready to accept it and think of the happy things.

As I dreamed I reminisced of the good times of our travels, the times of sharing, praying together as friends and living and working together as a family unit. I took comfort in the unity of huddling together as we walked through total darkness. We were like pioneers searching for a new land where things would be better and there would once again be sunlight and the world would be filled with other people.

Every one of us developed such a strong closeness as friends. We could only call our time together blessed. We did not have the everyday disruptions of daily living that we once had when our lives were normal. After the darkness occurred all we had left was each other, and we were forced to build strong ties together. Much stronger ties than any other bond we had ever had before in our lives. We had to learn to love each other and to get along, because our companionship was all that we had left. We could not survive the darkness without the connection with the other people in our group. That kind of closeness is something that every person yearns for, but few ever receive.

I loved cooking meals together and always eating dinner with our friends. None of us were ever left out or left alone. There was always someone close by to talk to or share ideas with. We had to have someone nearby at all times because we were afraid of being alone in the darkness. We developed genuine friendships that we could have never experienced in our everyday lives if the darkness hadn't occurred.

Cleaning up after dinner was so much easier with all of us working jointly. I have such heartwarming memories of our travels through the darkness. My thoughts were content as I dreamed about my friends. I slept that night in unconditional peace.

SEVEN

Life Goes On

The next day I went out to the garage to look for the old newspapers that my friend had given me after my accident. We were going over to my sister's at 6:00 to have dinner and watch the Boise State game, but I decided to search through some of the old newspapers again before it was time to leave. I had read through all of the papers when I first got out of the hospital, but it was time for me to read them again. Only this time I would carefully take the time to read each paragraph on every page.

I was healthier now and my mind was clearer. I decided I would study each page thoroughly and try to see if there was anything that could help me get the events of my accident straightened out. Perhaps the newspaper articles had put different ideas into my head when I read them last time and if I read the articles again I could get my thoughts sorted out and everything would start to make sense.

I spent hours rummaging through the old newspapers in the garage. We heated our house with wood so we used newspapers every day during the winter season. We had several boxes organized into piles ready to start the fireplace now that the weather was getting colder. I loved sitting in front of the fireplace every evening. It was so relaxing and comforting. In fact I was saddened every year when the fireplace season came to an end.

I had a lot of boxes to go through and I had to sort through every box searching the dates at the top of every paper. I finally located the box that had the papers that my friend had given me. The newspapers that I wanted were the dates starting on the day after my accident occurred and then continuing on for the several weeks following.

By the time I picked out all of the papers that I wanted to read I was tired. I brought the stacks of papers into the house and placed them on the end of the couch so that I could go through them after I took a short break and got me a fresh cup of coffee. I knew that reading all of them again was going to take me many hours and I wanted to rest for a few minutes before I got started.

I felt so much stronger than I did the first time that I read them. My mind was calmer and I knew that I would see things this time that I hadn't noticed the first time.

A few minutes later with a cup of hot coffee in hand I began sorting through the old newspapers again. I started with the newspaper that was published the day after my accident. This time I carefully read all of the details that were written about the young couple that had died. Their names were Margi and Gary Lambert of Meridian, Idaho.

Margi was a kindergarten teacher at Silver Sage Elementary School and the article said that Gary owned a printing shop in Meridian called Lambert's Printing where he made professional banners and posters. The couple was up in Garden Valley celebrating their second wedding anniversary.

As I looked over the next page I once again read about the power shortage that was predicted across the United States. The article was titled "The Day of the Darkness has begun." This article did not frighten me like it did the first time that I had read it, because I had also heard about the shortage mentioned on the television news only a few days ago. The announcement told about how over-crowded some of the larger cities were getting and how they just couldn't keep up with the demand for electricity. The newspaper said they didn't know exactly how long the current power source could provide enough power for all the multitudes of people that needed electricity.

The government was heavily pushing the wind turbines that we could see cropping up all across the United States. This time I stopped to read the complete article written about the wind turbines and the day of the darkness. Apparently, there was a lot of controversy as to the effectiveness of the wind energy and there appeared to be a lot of problems stemming from all of the giant wind turbines.

The article was really interesting though, it said that one of the leading sources to replace fossil fuels is also one of the oldest sources...the wind. The wind has been harnessed for centuries to mill grains and power ships and as far back as the 1930's it has been used to generate electricity.

Over the past 40 years as demand for power and the price of energy has steadily increased, so too have the efforts to turn wind into a viable option for producing electricity on a large scale. The potential of wind turbines, which convert kinetic energy into electric energy, has been promoted at every turn.

But there are a few risks. These wind turbines can be colossal, measuring more than 300 feet tall, weighing in at close to 400 tons, and equipped with rotating blades that may span 300 feet or more. And even the most ambitious plan from the US Department of energy aims to supply just 6 percent of the nation's electricity from wind by the year 2020. They are questioning if it is worth it.

Subsidies and incentives offered by the government are creating a sense of urgency for utility providers and co-ops to install wind farms. Wind energy is a cost-intensive operation.

Constructing a 50 megawatt wind farm (around 25 wind turbines) carries an up-front cost of around $65 million, and that's before a single kilowatt of electricity is generated. That seems pretty expensive for something as unpredictable as the wind.

The article went on to say that wind is a form of solar energy and it is a result of the uneven heating of the atmosphere by the sun, the irregularities of the earth's surface and the rotation of the earth. Wind flow patterns and speeds vary greatly across the Untied States and are modified by bodies of water, vegetation and the difference in terrain. Humans use the wind flow or motion energy for many purposes: like sailing, flying kites and of course generating electricity.

The term wind energy or wind power describes the process by which the wind is used to generate mechanical power or electricity. Wind turbines convert the kinetic energy in the wind into mechanical power. The mechanical power can be used for specific tasks; such as grinding grain or pumping water or a generator can convert this mechanical power into electricity.

So how do wind turbines make electricity? Simply stated a wind turbine works the opposite of a fan. Instead of using electricity to make wind like a fan, wind turbines use wind to make electricity. The wind turns the blades, which spin the shaft, which connects to a generator and makes electricity.

Each turbine requires approximately 150 acres per turbine. They must be placed in sweeping mountain ranges or breezy coastlines. Either place is ideal for both wind farms and tourists, but some communities do not want wind farms out of fear that the tourist will not come any longer.

Also, many people have complained that there is a light constant humming sound. There have been reported problems similar to the symptoms as Sick Building Syndrome. The condition that plagued office workers in the eighties and nineties as a result of what was eventually discovered to be Low Frequency Noise (LFN) caused by misdiagnosed air conditioner systems. It is sometime referred to as Amplified Modulation or loudness that goes up and down.

Some economists say that wind energy is unreliable and intermittent with no real market value because it requires nearly 100 percent back up by conventional fossil fuel power.

Another complaint about the huge machines is that each turbine kills around 300 birds a year. Oftentimes they are rare birds like eagles and also many bats.

"We have quite a few of the wind turbines here in Idaho," I said talking to myself. "There are a lot of them over near Pocatello where our friends live. In fact I think they add more and more turbines to their wind farm every time I go over that direction."

I shook my head back and forth and kind of shivered as I recalled the enormous monster-looking structures that completely saturated that whole region. "All you can see for miles are the huge turbines covering the entire canyon in every direction." I thought about them for a minute and I felt kind of uneasy, "Actually, those giant turbines are kind of intimidating, they sort of remind you of aliens from outer-space; especially when you are driving through the area around sunset, right before dark."

I covered my eyes and rubbed my forehead and I knew it was time to move to another paper. I finished reading the rest of that day's newspaper and I was getting very tired of reading. I had completely had my fill of reading old newspaper articles for one day. I had carefully read every single article on every page. I didn't want to miss anything that could be of any importance to me, but I was done for the day.

I slowly got up from the couch and stretched. It had been a long productive day of searching, but I needed to get ready to go watch football at my sister's. Darrell had fixed finger sandwiches, a chocolate cake and my favorite, macaroni salad. He was almost ready to go, so I knew it was time for me to put all of the newspapers down and get dressed.

We always went to my sister's for the Boise State games to have dinner and watch football on her giant screen TV. She bought a huge TV so that she could have friends over to watch the game every week. We had been going over there for every game for the past couple of years.

I put on my blue and orange Boise State sweatshirt and some clean Levi's and I was ready to go. My husband had loaded all of the food into the car and we were off.

Kick-off was in thirty minutes and my sister lived about ten minutes away so we should have plenty of time to get there and get settled before the game started. For three hours and 16 minutes we ate and focused on our favorite college football team. To me watching a good football game is like watching your favorite chic flick. It was a great game with one of our strongest rivals...Nevada, but we won 34 to 24. Yea, go Broncos!

We got home around 10:30 that night. I checked my e-mails on the computer and then we were off to bed. As I turned off the lights I glanced at the stacks of newspapers patiently waiting for my return. "I will get back to you in the morning," I whispered to the endless piles of papers.

EIGHT

Read On

The next day I changed the sheets on the bed and finished washing two loads of laundry before I sat down to get into the newspapers again. The front page told of people on food stamps, unemployment and movie stars visiting the white house and then I moved on to other articles.

I carefully read through the article talking about the masses of dead black birds that were piled around a camp ground up near Crouch. Witnesses had told how the birds just went crazy and rammed into each other before falling to their death. Those same witnesses told about a loud boom that had occurred around the same time. The witnesses thought the boom might have been what caused the birds to go so crazy and crash into each before falling to ground dead.

41

As I sat there reading the newspaper I distinctly recalled the dead black birds falling to the ground up at the restaurant in Garden Valley the night of my accident. Garden Valley and Crouch are within a few miles of each other. In fact many people think they are the same place.

Hearing about the dead birds is just one more similarity to tie that evening together with the time that my injury happened and the time that the day of the darkness occurred. After pondering over the article about the dead birds for several minutes I decided it was time to go on to another paper. I had carefully read every sentence on every page.

After painstakingly reading one page after another I came to the article about the truck driver that had crashed on the Horseshoe Bend hill. The driver was driving a big moving van down the steep Horseshoe Bend incline and he started traveling too fast. Witnesses behind the van said that the driver lost control of the van and began to swerve back and forth. The witnesses also said that he appeared to have lost his brakes and after shifting down he over-corrected and by the third corner he was going so fast that he rolled the van over and over again. As the van rolled it threw furniture up and down the entire highway stopping traffic on both sides of the road for several hours.

The article said that the van driver was killed at the scene of the accident. It said that the driver was a 39 year old male named Phillip Harding. He had worked for the Mairfield Moving Company out of Ontario, Canada for over seven years.

"What a tragic accident," I thought. "Those poor witnesses that were driving behind him must have been scared to death watching all of that happening right before their eyes. If he was from Canada maybe he hadn't ever been on the Horseshoe Bend Hill before and he didn't know how steep it was. That steep stretch of highway 55 has several run-away truck ramps."

I thought back to the night of the accident and once again my mind started to wander, "I was told that I was life-flighted back to Boise by helicopter. Yet, I unmistakably remember all of us driving the motorcycles back from Garden Valley."

"I will never forget driving through the devastating darkness," I murmured to myself. "I don't think I have ever been as afraid in my whole life as I was that night. The darkness, the silence and isolation was almost too much to endure," I recalled. My mind began to drift as I recalled the frightening ride home to Boise that terrifying evening. We traveled through hundreds of wrecked vehicles and past all of the abandoned houses and farms.

I closed my eyes to help shut out the images, but I could clearly see them inside my head. There were gigantic piles of debris scattered everywhere up and down the steep Horseshoe Bend Hill. Trash, glass, furniture; the motorcycles had to literally crawl over the massive litter and garbage that covered the abrupt hillside.

I stood up to take a break because everything was becoming so overwhelmingly real. I walked into the kitchen and poured myself a glass of milk with ice cubes. As I was standing there resting my brain and drinking my glass of milk my husband walked into the house carrying the telescope. "Hey look what I just found in the trailer," he commented looking very puzzled. "How do you think it got into the motorcycle trailer?"

I just shrugged my shoulders and shook my head because I knew there was no way that he would understand. We had used the telescope every day on our journey through the darkness. He would set the telescope up on the roof of a building or point it out a top story windowsill so that we could get our bearings to see which direction the daylight was. Then we would load up the motorcycles and trailers and head off towards the light.

Every day we got closer and closer to reaching the light because of the telescope guiding our way. But I knew that he wouldn't understand, so I just shrugged my shoulders and tried to look as confused as he did.

I finished my milk and decided to take a walk outside to try to clear my brain for awhile. Although, I felt much stronger than I did a week ago many of the questionable activities that had happened in Garden Valley were still very confusing to me. Most things made no sense what-so-ever.

I do remember the masses of black birds, but then after that everything in the stories began to disagree. The people who were there with us that night said that I was flown to Boise by helicopter, yet I remember driving back on the motorcycle after the darkness occurred. And there have been too many odd things happen in the past few days to show that there is truth in both recollections.

I know that I woke up in the hospital eight weeks ago, after being in a coma since June. I know that the same doctor had been taking care of me while I was in the hospital and he just released me a few weeks ago so that had to be real. And of course I read about my accident in Garden Valley in the newspaper and I know that two people from Meridian were killed that night; Margi and Gary Lambert.

But I also know that I got my giant lantern back and I hadn't ever loaned it to anyone. And I know that I found my beautiful black sweater in the drawer that I bought in Kansas, the one that is just like Darlene's sweater. I know that someone returned our old coffee pot and I had never loaned that to anyone either.

I also received one of the yellow IOU's in the mail from Evanston, Wyoming and I have never been to Evanston, Wyoming except on our journey through the darkness. Then of course my husband discovered the telescope in our motorcycle trailer and we have never taken the telescope in the trailer before.

There are too many questions with too many complicated answers; so I must ask myself if any of the answers really matter. Today there is sunlight and the day of the darkness has passed. I am no longer in a coma in the hospital and I still have all of my family and friends so, I must be thankful for both answers.

My brain was on over-load so I took a break to fix lunch. After fixing a ham and cheese sandwich and a cup of tomato soup for my husband and me it was time to move on through the rest of the newspapers. I was anxious to get through all of them. I put the lunch dishes in the sink and got me a fresh cup of coffee and then I sat down to search through the old papers once again.

I read about the load of lumber that had covered the freeway over near Twin Falls, but the article that caught my attention was the one about the Great Salt Lake. It told in detail how the Salt Lake had flooded for the first time in several generations.

I considered all of the things that had happened, "Okay," I thought. "Someone brought back our coffee pot with a note attached and left it on the front deck. The note said that they had been scrubbing the dried white saltwater powder off of their trailer for two days," I muttered to myself trying to make sense of everything.

Once again I could vividly picture the raging waters of the Great Salt Lake. The intimidating flood waters got higher and higher as they tried to overpower our bikes and trailers as we traveled on the Interstate on our way to Salt Lake City. It was difficult for us to understand that the usually peaceful Salt Lake was continually rising and it would soon reach an unimaginable flood stage.

The water had persistently gotten deeper until it had spread out covering the total area all the way across the plain and up to the mountains. I will never forget that panicky feeling of being stranded in the middle of the flooding black river in absolute darkness, it was terrifying beyond words.

I shook my head back and forth trying to clear my thoughts and I decided it was time to move on. I continued to read the articles of the following days. I was relieved to find nothing that pertained to my life.

I glanced through the piece about the volcano in Colorado, but the one main article that caught my interest was the article about the huge fire. The merciless inferno had burned across four states and it took several weeks to get it under control.

Once again my mind drifted off as I remembered the giant fire that we had spent days trying to get around when we were on our extended journey through the darkness. It was because of the raging fire that we were forced to double back and try to drive far enough around the fire storm so that we could travel up towards Chicago.

That was when we found the old deserted farmhouse. At first we felt lucky to have a place to spend the night, but it wasn't until we woke up eight hours later that we discovered the blood and boarded up windows in the upstairs attic. I knew it was the same abandoned farmhouse that the newspaper article had written about. Because the article had pictures and I could recognize the pictures of the inside of the house; even if we had to use our flashlights to light up each room, it still looked exactly the way that I had remembered it. I recognized the old wallpaper.

After completely reading every sentence on every page of every newspaper I came to the article about the snowstorm in Atlanta. I shivered as I remembered the deep freezing snow that started to fall when we drove into the motel in Atlanta. Snow and motorcycles do not do well together. I remember being trapped inside the motel for several days as the snow continued to fall and the weather got colder and colder with each passing hour.

I remember sleeping under piles and piles of blankets and sleeping bags. I closed my eyes as I recalled how cozy I felt. I was so comfortable that I never wanted to get up.

Next thing that I remembered I woke up at Saint Alphonsus Hospital and I was told that I had been in a coma for several weeks.

NINE

As the World Turns

It was time to put all of the old newspapers back into the box so that they could one day be used to start the fireplace, but not just yet. I wanted to keep these particular newspapers for a little while longer. For some reason they were my security. They were my only real tie that bound the day of the darkness with my accident in Garden Valley.

I hid the box with my special newspapers back in the corner of my closet so that no one would ever question me about them. I had read them from beginning to end, line by line, but I felt I needed to keep them nearby in case I ever wanted to look at them again. So, I covered the small box of papers with an old blanket and closed the closet door.

Then I neatly folded the note pad paper that I had been writing all of my notes on and I put it in one of the side pockets of my purse. I wanted to keep it in a safe place where I could get to it and look it over if I ever needed to.

It was time to fix dinner for my husband so I fixed pork chops, green beans and mashed potatoes and gravy. We had a fresh green salad and I made Darrell's favorite...hot crescent rolls.

While we were sipping our coffee after dinner and having a bowl of vanilla bean ice cream we talked about Darrek's next game. It was an out-of-town game in McCall and we planned to go. I had made reservations at the Holiday Inn Express so that we wouldn't have to drive home late at night after the game. We both were excited about getting away for a couple of days and McCall is always a great place to go. It was still a little early for snow, but the fall colors should be beautiful this time of year.

The Cole Valley Christian Chargers won the game 42 -7, it was a great game for our side, but we felt kind of sorry for the McCall team. It was so cold and we about froze to death, but it was worth the trip. It was so much colder up in the mountains than it was down in Boise. Even wrapped up in blankets we were all freezing.

After the game we went out to the Toll House pizza with the team and all of the parents. The restaurant is up a small hill and off to the right with the huge parking lot. It is the place where everybody goes to have pizza when they are in McCall.

We had a large group of hungry football players and their families, but I had to commend the management because they did a fantastic job of quickly feeding all of us and getting us out the door.

Some of the football players who didn't have parents at the game in McCall were riding the bus back to Boise that night and they needed to get on their way home before it got too late. As the players walked out the door to load the bus I went and sat in the car to wait until my family was ready to go back to the motel.

My husband went over with our son to say goodbye to the players on the bus and to remind them again of what a good game they had all played. None of the guys on the bus had their families up there at the game. And many of the adults that were up there in McCall were getting on the bus for a few minutes and being stand-in parents and grandparents and encouraging the team about their game before they headed home.

All of the families at the school were a close knit group and they always encouraged each team player. Oftentimes parents shouted out to our grandson as we left games. Everyone knew each other and the adults easily talked to all of the kids.

As I watched the players loading onto the bus I noticed a large moving van that was parked right next to the bus. The name on the moving van took me by surprise because it was the same name that I had just read about in one of the old newspapers a few days ago. It was the Mairfield Moving Company and it was the same kind of large moving van that had crashed and rolled down the Horseshoe Bend Hill in June.

I reached inside my purse and pulled out the note pad sheet to verify the information on the moving van and I was right, this was part of the same company. I carefully read over all of the information about the accident and then I placed the paper back inside my purse.

I felt such a strong connection to this company, because the truck driver had his accident around the same time that I had my accident in Garden Valley.

Seeing the large moving van parked there in McCall once again made me think of that fateful night last June. Even when I close my eyes I could clearly see that evening just like it happened yesterday. I distinctly remember the loud boom and the fireball coming down from the sky creating a massive glow that lit up the entire mountainside and when it disappeared everything went black. The sun, the moon, even the stars had vanished. "I know that it really happened," I whispered out loud.

"I will never forget traveling home after the darkness had occurred. Not knowing what caused the darkness in the first place and fearing that an enemy might be lurking out in the shadows; just watching and waiting because he could see us, but we couldn't see him. I remember driving through the unknown, driving past abandoned cars, motor homes and houses. I was so terrified," I whispered to myself.

My deep thoughts were interrupted when my husband knocked on the car door and motioned for me to unlock the door so that he could get in. We drove to the motel and had freshly baked chocolate cookies and coffee with our kids and grandkids and then it was off to bed. We were all really exhausted.

As I tried to fall asleep I once again reminded myself, "Everything in this world does not have to make sense."

We got up around 7:00 a.m. the next morning and ate breakfast downstairs at the motel at 8:00 and then we headed back to Boise.

As we climbed up the steep Horseshoe Bend Hill I studied the section where the newspaper report stated that the Mairfield Moving van had crashed and rolled. It had been several months since the accident had occurred, but I saw no sign of any mishap.

The football game was great and I am so glad that we went to McCall for Darrek's game, but I had mixed feelings after seeing the large moving van. It brought back all of the things that I had been trying so hard to forget.

It was becoming very clear to me that something abnormal had happened up in Garden Valley the night that I had my accident; something strange and unexplainable, because too many unusual occurrences had happened that didn't make any sense. I knew that somehow I had to learn to ignore all of the peculiar things that I could not understand. I must accept them rather than try to find a reason for their happenings.

TEN

We Love Our Grandkids

Early Monday morning I got up and got dressed and decided it was time to go out shopping alone. I felt healthier and much stronger. No matter what strange things had happened in the past few weeks I knew it was it time for me to get out and start living again. Before my accident I was so independent I went everywhere by myself. If I had serious shopping to get done I always went alone, because I got more accomplished when I was on my own.

But I have not been out by myself since before my accident. My husband always drives me everywhere that I need to go. I think he is afraid to let me get out of his sight. He has been through so much in the past several months, he oftentimes coddles me.

53

I have to realize that when you sit at the bedside of your injured wife, not knowing if she will live or die your whole outlook on life begins to change. You sort out what is important and what is not a priority. I think that is why he doesn't question many of the things that I do anymore. Before the accident he would have questioned me about everything, but now he just lets things pass.

Even as I got myself around and got ready to go I knew that he was going to have a very difficult time letting me get out of the house alone. I have no idea what he fears will happen to me, but I know that he has rarely let me out of his sight for very long since my accident.

If he actually knew the things that I see, hear and dream he would really have something to be worried about. I have had so many odd things happen to me since I have recovered from my accident, and yet I have to keep everything hidden inside of my head.

I'm sure my husband sees me as being very fragile since my accident, but actually I am probably stronger than I ever have been in my life. I know that I am keeping a lot more secrets from everyone than I ever did before. I am a much more private person since I had my accident. I have to be because my brain is filled with so many unanswered questions.

Today will be the first time that I have actually been out of the house by myself since the time of the darkness. It is strange to think how different the world appears when there is light. To once again have electricity, sunlight, moonlight and stars. What a wonderful gift the Lord gave us when he gave us the gift of sunlight. I will never again take it for granted.

I love the sunshine. Before my accident one of my favorite things to do was to sit in a chair in the middle of the yard and close my eyes and just feel the warm sun on my face.

I also loved to meet friends for lunch and just visit for hours. We would have a leisurely lunch and then we would browse through one of the local gift shops. Visiting with friends has always been one of my favorite things in life. Maybe soon I will be brave enough to go out with a friend and then go shopping through a crowded novelty store, but not today. Today I am on my own. Today I must once again learn to walk alone.

I have to get my life straightened out because we have so many things that we need to do in the next week. Our oldest grandson Michael plays in a band called *My Young Dreamer* and tonight he will be playing at a fund raiser for one of his friends who drowned in the river a few months ago. And of course we plan to go to that.

Tuesday night we will have to miss our CMA dinner group because our grandson Devon has a choir performance at Cole Valley Christian. Wednesday night is Bible Study night and Thursday night our granddaughter Hailie has a ballet performance at the NNU auditorium and she is one of the lead performers.

Friday night our seven year old granddaughter, Kennedy will take turns with the tee dog at the Boise State game retrieving the kicking tee.

Kennedy is a long-distance runner, just like her parents and she was chosen to be the Zamzow's kicking tee retriever for this home game. It is quite an honor to be the child that runs out on the field to retrieve the tee. So, Friday night we will go to the Boise State game and cheer on our number 5 grandchild as she retrieves the kicking tee.

Saturday night Darrek has another Cole Valley Christian game and we will take the three youngest grandkids with us to the game. That's why I need to go out shopping and put together three little gift sacks for our three grandkids to play with at the game.

Darrell and I love taking our grandkids places with us and we don't get them often enough. Since my accident I have missed out on several months of play. So, Saturday night we get Kennedy, Greyson and Emerson to ourselves at the football game. Grandma and Grandpa will feel like they are in heaven.

With seven grandchildren this is just a regular week for us. That is why I must get out on my own so that my world can get back to normal.

I casually walked in and kissed my husband goodbye and told him that I was going to go out for awhile. He said just what I expected him to say, "Oh honey, I can take you. Where do you need to go?"

I smiled at him and tried to let him down easy as I said, "No it is time for me to get out on my own. I am healthy, I have my strength back and it is time for me to go out by myself for awhile."

He could tell there was no changing my mind. I needed to fully recuperate from my accident and getting out into the world for a few minutes alone was the only way that I was going to recover. I had to start by taking baby steps.

He nodded his head and smiled and told me, "O.K. but you be careful."

When I got into the car I felt panic for a second because reality hit me. I was really going to do this. I knew that I would soon be out in the world all by myself. The warm sunlight felt wonderful as it filtered in through the front window of the car. Even with the air getting colder outside Boise still enjoyed sunlight almost every single day and the sunlight gave me courage.

I drove down to Fred Meyers and I walked around the store picking out little goodies to put in the bags for my three precious grandkids for the football game this weekend. I found small color books, sketch pads and new boxes of felt pens and multicolored stickers for each gift bag.

I also bought two large bags of tootsie roll pop suckers to give to our grandson Devon to hand out to his friends while we were all at the game. I often bought bags of candy for Devon to share with his friends.

It actually felt great to be out shopping again. It was amazing to be out amongst people and to be able to walk around like a regular person as if nothing traumatic had ever happened in my life.

I saw several people that I knew and we would visit for a couple of minutes and then I would get back to my shopping. I had made it. I was out alone and everything was all right.

I was towards the back of the store and I was just heading to the check stand when everything in the store went black...the power went out. I could feel my heart racing and it was very hard to breath. I stood perfectly still; because I was too terrified to move.

This was not the first time that I had been in this store in the dark. I was in this same store twice during the time of darkness; once alone with my husband Darrell and the second time with all of our friends as we were preparing to leave on our long journey towards the light.

The reason that we were able to get into this store when the power was out is because the automatic front doors were left wide open as if someone was walking through them at the time the darkness occurred. The automatic doors just remained open indefinitely. We knew that we could get into this store and that is why we all chose to come here as we prepared for our travels. This was the first place that we had left a yellow IOU paper.

Within a few seconds I was jarred back to reality as someone came running past me with a huge flashlight. "Are you all right?" the man asked me as he scurried by.

"Yes, I'm fine," I answered the store manger as he headed off towards the front of the store.

Suddenly I heard voices coming from all around me. Many people turned on their cell phones for light, while others took small keychain flashlights out of their pockets and purses. I heard one woman shout to her kids that someone had hit the power pole out in the intersection and it had destroyed all of the power for several blocks.

"The power pole," I said to myself over and over. "It is only the power pole." In a few minutes we heard sirens outside and they were coming from every direction.

The emergency power system came on and it was as if the power had never been off. I went up to the check stand and paid for my items and walked out to my car to go home. I sat in my car for a few seconds and caught my breath and thanked the Lord that I had been able to remain calm even in a time of panic. "I survived," I congratulated myself, I had survived.

As I pulled out into the street I saw my husband driving towards me in his red Dodge truck. He rolled down his window and shouted, "Are you all right, I heard all of the sirens."

I smiled and shook my head up and down, "Yes, I'm fine I'll meet you at home." I had to chuckle as I drove on down Overland Road talking to myself, "I wonder if he will be like this from now on?"

ELEVEN

The Winds

Our life was finally back to normal. We had made it through Halloween, Thanksgiving, Christmas, Valentine's Day and Easter.

Nothing else unusual had taken place so I was sure that the mysteries of Garden Valley were now over. It was late May and the weather was warm and beautiful and our life was getting back into a regular routine. We had taken several short rides with our friends from the motorcycle group and everything was good. I had adjusted to being by myself in the car, the store and the mall. I could go anywhere alone. I felt sure that my world was finally straightened out and that I had gotten a firm grip on life.

Most people had completely forgotten about my accident because it had happened last June, almost a year ago and I appeared so healthy. Few people even asked me about my accident anymore and that was fine with me. I wanted to move on and live the rest of my life as if the controversy of the day of the darkness had never happened.

One morning as I was reading the newspaper I read about some unusual wind storms that they were having in a small town over near Pocatello, Idaho. The article caught my attention because we have good friends that live in that area and we go over and see them all of the time.

The editorial said that the violent wind gust had been so ruthless that they had ruined entire fields during the planting season. The article compared the strong winds in the area to the dust bowl of the 1930's. In the 1930's many crops were ruined by deficient rainfall, high temperatures and severe winds.

Our friends that moved there were from our motorcycle group. They sold their property in Boise and bought a small farm over there a couple of years ago. They loved the area and they had family that lived in that vicinity and so they moved there to be closer to their family.

The article in the newspaper said that the local residents were baffled by the problems that the massive wind storms were creating. The people that live in the surrounding area are used to it being windy, but for some reason the wind storms seem to be getting stronger every day.

The farmers are complaining that the terrible winds are destroying the top soil. They are afraid that they won't be able to grow their crops this year because the violent winds are so brutal and the wind continually blows the seeds and soil away. Many people are saying that after a full week of the violent winds the entire town is slowly being destroyed.

When the winds come up the visibility is only a few feet and it makes for very hazardous driving conditions. Within a few short days the roads have become cluttered with trash, dirt and fallen trees. So the traffic advisors have told people to stay off of the roads as much as possible.

They have also been telling people to stay inside during the daytime as often as they can until the authorities can figure out exactly what is causing the violent wind storms. They have advised people to only go outside after sunset, because for some odd reason the winds stop completely during the night time. So far there have been no serious car accidents caused by the winds, but they are strongly advising people not to drive or use any farm equipment until the warning is lifted.

The blowing dust is causing severe eye irritations and upper respiratory problems. The surrounding hospitals have been over-crowded with people struggling with asthma and breathing machines. The local health department has advised people to wear a dust mask at all times. The Red Cross is giving away free boxes of dust masks every evening at all of the Walgreen's and Rite Aide stores in Pocatello, Chubbuck and American Falls.

The local news said that meteorologists have not been able to figure out what is causing the severe wind gusts, because the strong winds do not go with the weather patterns. Something else is driving the relentless winds and it has nothing to do with the weather. They have brought in several wind and weather science specialists to evaluate the direct cause of the blustery dry winds, but so far they have not reported anything significant.

Two people are presumed dead after the wind destroyed their barn and a large portion of their farmhouse. Franklin and Josephine Faber have been missing for several days and authorities believe that they are buried beneath the rubble of their old barn along with their two horses and a goat. The local sheriff said that the wind completely demolished their barn and it destroyed most of their house, but the strong winds have kept the volunteers from retrieving the bodies. The rural farmhouse is located in Tower County where the winds appear to be the most severe.

The report also said that several farmers had found many of their cattle dead after putting them out on the open range for the season. One farmer reported as many as 200 head of cattle were found mysteriously killed out by the massive wind farm near the Snake River Canyon area.

The dead cattle were all covered with bites or stings from some kind of insect. Many of the cattle had been dead for days by the time the farmers could finally get to them, but the severe gusty winds have prevented the farmers from locating their cows very quickly because of such horrible visibility. Only when the winds subside at night have the farmers been able to use flood lights and locate the lifeless animals.

The report said that the lab results are inconclusive on the type of insect that could be killing the cattle. So far there have been no reports of any humans or other animals affected by the bites, but the doctors are advising the area residents to keep their families and pets inside the house as much as possible.

The town's people are scared because there are too many unusual things going on between the violent winds and the killer insects. Many parents have refused to send their children to school because of all of the strange occurrences. So, the authorities are trying to decide if they need to close all of the schools until the scientists and the meteorologists can figure out what is causing the weird phenomenon around that region.

"What is going on over there," I thought. "This sounds like something out of a terror movie. I need to call our friends; they must be worried to death."

I fixed myself a cup of hot tea and then I sat down to contact our friends. I hadn't talked to them for a couple of weeks and I usually talked with them at least once a week, and sometimes every day if we have something planned.

The four of us had been friends for years. Suzanne was like a sister to me, we told each other everything. Our friendship began over forty years ago when we all started riding together to the motorcycle rallies. Our husbands were good friends and our kids were around the same age and they had all grown up together. We had gone to the same church and our families planned yearly camping trips. They were some of the closet friends that we had ever had and we missed them terribly since they had moved away.

It has been a little over two years ago since they moved to the Pocatello area, and they keep telling everyone how much they love living there. They said it is so quiet and peaceful and everyone is so friendly, they just love the community.

We were surprised how quickly they adjusted to the move, because they had lived in Boise for as long as we had known them. Then one day they had a huge garage sale and sold half of their stuff and they took off and never looked back.

They bought a lot of new furniture when they moved to their small farm. I'm sure it was really hard for them to pack up and leave, but they have seemed really happy, so maybe it was a lot harder for us to have them move away, than it was for them.

We couldn't believe it because on one Sunday afternoon as we were all out to lunch; they told us the devastating news that they had put their house up for sale. Their plan to move over near Pocatello had taken us by total surprise, because we did things with them all of the time and we had no idea that they planned to move away. We didn't know anything about it until that day. They had gone over to visit family several times, so maybe we should have suspected something, but we never thought they would actually move away after living in Boise for all of these years.

A month after they put their house up for sale...it sold and we helped them move everything that they had left to their quiet little farm over in Tower County. It was so beautiful over there, I could see why they wanted to move there, but I was just sick. I hate changes, so I was sick for weeks after they moved, in fact it stills makes me sad to think about it.

Many of our friends from the motorcycle group have gone over to see them since they moved away. It is very hard to move from the area where you have always lived. But my friend Suzanne loves her yard and her garden. They have a nice little farm and it really isn't that far from Boise.

The more I thought about our friends the more anxious I became. The newspaper article made their situation sound so dire, and I could hardly wait to get a hold of them. "I'm sure things aren't as bad as the paper makes it sound," I assured myself. But when I finally did reach my friend the connection was so terrible that I could barely understand her. Apparently the strong winds were affecting the phone lines and making the reception really poor.

My heart was breaking as I talked to my dear friend. She told me, "The conditions seem to be getting worse on a daily basis. The whole situation is so strange because the horrible winds didn't even start until the weather started to get warmer. But once the weather got warm the gusts just got stronger and stronger every day," she told me. "Our condition is much worse than you can even imagine." She paused before going on, "It is so scary here; half of the roof blew off of our house during a wind gust yesterday and it is so bad you can see daylight from the upstairs bedroom."

"But there is nothing we can do to fix it unless we fix it at night because we can't even go outside during the daytime," she complained. "I just lock the upstairs bedroom door and don't go up there." My dear friend sounded so upset I knew she was about to cry then she said, "All day long we feel like we are in the center of a tornado and it never stops."

We didn't talk very long because the telephone reception was so bad and I could hear the wind howling in the background. "Tell Gene that we are thinking of him," I shouted into the phone. "You will be in our thoughts and prayers. I will call you in a few days to check and see if things are getting better," I told her as I was hanging up. I could barely hear her say goodbye, before the line went dead.

After I hung up I sat there and thought about our good friends. Even with the terrible phone reception I could tell she was really frightened. I felt so scared for her I wished there was something that I could do to help her.

"Strong winds really frighten me too," I thought. "I don't mind heavy rain, snowstorms or the cold, but strong winds scare me more than anything. I can't imagine it blowing all of the time and never stopping. But she said they do stop, they stop at night; why do they stop at night?" I questioned.

"The whole thing seems really eerie to me," I commented out loud. "Oh, I forgot to ask her about the insects. That is really odd because most insects don't like the wind. I wonder why the insects would be biting the animals when it is so windy. The entire situation seems so troubling no wonder Suzanne sounds so distraught," I said talking to myself. "I'll call her in a day or so and see if things are getting better."

TWELVE

Idaho History

My mind began to wander as I sat there drinking my tea. As I thought about Suzanne and Gene I thought about some of the other things that have happened over by where they live.

Several years ago the towns of Rexburg and Sugar City were almost flooded off of the map because of the Teton Dam disaster. When the Teton Dam was being constructed it was supposed to be the greatest dam that was ever built. The Teton Dam was a new earth filled dam located between Freemont County and Madison County. The water from the dam was to be used to generate hydroelectric power.

But on Saturday June 5, 1976 at 7:30 a.m. (MDT) as they were filling the new dam with water for the very first time a muddy leak appeared suggesting that sediment was in the water. By 11:55 a.m. the dam collapsed sending over 2,000,000 cubic feet per second of sediment-filled water downstream resulting in the deaths of 11 people and 13,000 head of cattle. The water flowed out into the remaining six miles of the Teton River Canyon, after which the flood spread out and swallowed up the surrounding farm land.

The small community of American Falls is nestled along the edge of the Snake River and the reservoir serves as the business hub for Southeastern Idaho. The town of American Falls is several miles downstream from the Teton Dam site. They grow potatoes, grain and sugar beets and farming is the heart of the community, but they also depend on tourism.

The American Falls Dam is a concrete gravity type dam located near the heart of town on the Snake River in Tower County. The dam is used for flood control irrigation and recreation, but a few years ago when the Teton Dam disaster happened it almost destroyed the entire town of American Falls.

The first power plant at the falls was built in 1901. In 1927 the first dam was built which required the relocation of the whole town, including the buildings. A short distance to the southwest is where the original town site was, but it is now under water and an old concrete grain silo still sticks up out of the water marking the original site.

After the Teton Dam failed, the floodwaters struck several communities and immediately downstream thousands of homes and businesses were destroyed. The city of Rexburg with a population of around 10,000, at that time was almost totally destroyed, because 80% of the structures were under water.

Rick's College was one of the only buildings spared because it sat safely on top of a hill. Many of the residents of Rexburg had to spend the rest of that summer living in the college dorms because everything in the town had been inundated with water and sludge.

The mud was a serious problem because the town was directly down stream from the stockyards, the rodeo grounds, the saw mill and the fertilizer plant. It was important to get the wet mud off of everything before it dried because the valley soil is high in clay and the mud from the dam was made of a material intended to harden and set up. Many townspeople spent weeks cleaning up the sludge after the terrible flood.

A significant reason for the massive damage to the communities was the location of a lumber yard directly upstream when the flood hit. Thousands of logs were washed into the towns. Dozens of them hit gasoline storage tanks a few hundred yards away and the gasoline ignited and sent flaming sticks adrift on the raging water. The force of the logs and cut lumber and subsequent fires practically destroyed everything in its path.

At the older American Falls Dam downstream, engineers increased discharge by less than 5% before the flood arrived. The American Falls Dam held and the flood was effectively over, but tens of thousands of acres of fertile topsoil were destroyed.

The Teton Dam project cost about $100 million to build and the Federal Government ended up paying $322 million for 7,563 damage and death claims. In 1978 American Falls built a larger new dam and the old dam was demolished. The Teton Dam project was never rebuilt, but maybe it will be someday.

Pocatello was not really affected by the Teton Dam disaster, but Pocatello is only about 28 minutes away from American Falls. Pocatello is the county seat and it is the largest city in Bannock County with a small portion of the Fort Hall Indian Reservation in Tower County.

Pocatello is the 5th largest city in the state of Idaho just behind Idaho Falls.

In 1860 the discovery of Gold in Idaho brought the first large wave of U.S. settlers to the region. The Portneuf region became an important conduit for the transportation of goods.

In 1877 the main railroad acquired and extended the Utah and Nevada Railway which previously stopped in Utah.

The city of Pocatello was named after Chief Pocatello of the Shoshoni Indian Tribe, but the chief actually never called himself Chief Pocatello he called himself Tondzaosha a Shoshoni word for buffalo robe.

Nathaniel James Wyeth a fur trader established Fort Hall as a trading post just north of the present location of the city. It became an important stop on the Oregon Trail.

Pocatello absorbed nearby Alameda in 1962 and briefly became the largest city in Idaho, even ahead of Boise.

Pocatello gained attention in the 1954 musical film *A Star is Born*, in which Judy Garland sang the song "Born in a Trunk" about being born in the Princess Theatre in Pocatello, Idaho. Part of the 2006 film *Bonneville* occurs in Pocatello and, although it was not filmed in Idaho, actress Kathy Bates attended an LDS Church in Pocatello to research her character. Portions of the movie *Napoleon Dynamite* were filmed in Pocatello.

The city of Pocatello was ranked 20th in the nation on the Forbes List of best small places for Business and Career opportunities. It is the home of Idaho State University and the manufacturing facility of ON Semiconductors.

Actually, Idaho Falls is the largest city outside of the Boise metropolitan area. It is often listed as one of the "Best places to Live,"

But one of my favorite cities in the magic valley is Twin Falls, Idaho. In 1900 I. B. Perrine founded the Twin Falls Land and Water Company. He was granted the necessary water rights and that helped develop the entire Magic Valley. Twenty-four years later in 1924 the towering Perrine Bridge was built and thus named after I. B. Perrine. The bridge connects the city of Twin Falls to Jerome County. The Perrine Bridge is one of the only artificial structures in the world from which Base Jumping is legal. In 2005, Miles Dasher of Twin Falls set a world record by jumping off of the bridge 57 times in a 24 hour period.

There are three waterfalls in the immediate area. The most famous is the Shoshone Falls. Shoshone Falls is taller than Niagara Falls by 36 feet.

If you take the Scenic Byway from Twin Falls towards Buhl you'll discover "The Trout Capital of the World." Buhl has many hatcheries which promote a majority of the rainbow trout consumed in the Untied States. Clear Springs Foods located just north of Buhl processes over 20 million pounds of rainbow trout each year, making it the world's largest producer.

As you travel on down Route 30 or the scenic byway you come to Hagerman which is a town in Gooding County. The area is noted for its fossil beds and the Thousand Springs of the Eastern Snake River Plain Aquifer. Hagerman is also known for its alligator farms. The restaurant in downtown Hagerman actually serves fresh alligator on the menu every day.

Hagerman is the home of the Hagerman Fossil Beds National Monument of the U.S. National Park Service. More than 180 animal species of both vertebrates and invertebrates and 35 plant species have been found in the Hagerman fossil sites. Eight of the species are found nowhere else.

THIRTEEN

Safe-Haven

I was so concerned after I talked to Suzanne on the phone the first time, that I called her again a couple of days later. I could barely understand her because of all of the static and the blowing winds. She shouted as she told me, "My yard is completely destroyed, four of our huge old trees have blown over and we have moved some of our clothes and bedding downstairs to the basement. I have been busy most of the day moving all of our food and survival supplies downstairs because the house seems too unstable to stay upstairs."

I shouted back to her, "Why don't you guys leave when it gets dark tonight? As soon as the winds stop just pack up a few things and drive back to Boise. You can stay with us until all of this gets settled and the windstorms pass."

"A lot of our neighbors have already left," she shouted. "But we can't leave tonight so let me see about tomorrow night," she screamed trying to shout above the howling winds. "I'll call you tomorrow," she shouted as the line went dead.

"They are moving to the basement." I said to my husband. "This is crazy, I have never heard of such a thing."

"I didn't even know that they had a basement. Why are they staying in the basement?" my husband Darrell questioned.

"She said that the house was too unstable to stay upstairs," I told him shaking my head. Then I realized what he had asked me, "I wouldn't really say they have a basement. They just have a tiny one room storage area with a drop-down ladder that comes down out of the laundry room. It has concrete walls and it is unfinished. Actually it is more like a dark musty fruit cellar," I told him.

"Suzanne said they are moving downstairs because the winds are too strong, and they are afraid to stay upstairs. So they are moving some of their food and bedding downstairs." I answered halfway on the verge of tears. "This whole situation is so terrifying. They have got to get out of there. The wind has already destroyed her beautiful yard and it has even blown over four of their huge trees," I told him shaking my head back and forth.

Darrell got a puzzled look on his face as he said, "What if for some reason the winds never stop? What if it is not a seasonal thing? The meteorologist said it has nothing to do with the weather patterns. What will they do then? There is no way they can stay down in the basement all of the time and it sounds like the windstorms are getting worse every day," Darrell answered sounding almost as upset as I was.

"I know, I know," I commented. "This is just so scary I can't believe it. Oh Honey, she sounded so helpless," I told him as I covered my face to keep from crying, "We have got to get them out of there."

Darrell and I watched the ten o'clock news and again there was breaking news out of Tower County. The reporter said, "The situation in Tower County has gotten so severe that the police have put up roadblocks on the interstate. They are stopping everyone and making them turn around and go back to avoid going into the restricted area." He went on, "They call the turn around area the safe-haven position." He continued, "They are not allowing anyone to go beyond that point, because the region is no longer safe." He went on, "Roadblocks have also been posted on the Pocatello side so that people cannot enter Tower County from any direction."

"I can not believe this madness," I complained. "I have never in my life heard of the police blocking off an entire region and not letting anyone into the area because it is too windy. Not in Idaho! That is absolutely ludicrous," I ranted. "We have got to do something." I sat down and put my hands over my face, "I cannot understand how the conditions could have gotten this bad so quickly. In a little over ten days the entire area has become a total disaster."

My husband and I sat up and talked about their situation for a long time and then we finally went to bed about midnight, but I couldn't sleep. I had such a terrible feeling about our friends. I kept thinking about the way she sounded on the phone and every time that I'd close my eyes to try to sleep I would think that I could hear the wind howling outside. Turbulent blowing wind is such a disturbing sound and to be able to hear it even over the phone as we talked, was unreal.

I tossed and turned for hours; I could hardly wait until morning so that I could call her again and beg her to come back to Boise. I finally fell asleep and I woke up at 7:00.

I walked into the kitchen to start the coffee and then I went outside to get the newspaper. The front page article told about the appalling situation that was going on over in Tower County. The newspaper explained how the problems were getting worse each day and they still have not pinpointed the cause of the hurricane-type winds. The article explained how they have brought in weather scientists from as far away as China, Thailand, and India.

"What is going on over there?" I almost screamed out loud. "This is one of the weirdest things that I have ever heard of in my life and I can't believe it is happening right here in our state."

"Idaho rarely has tornadoes, floods, earthquakes or any type of emergency disaster. We have wind storms, but not severe winds that get stronger every single day. Then for some unforeseen reason they stop at night and began again the next day and they are worse than they were the day before. That is crazy," I screamed as I threw the newspaper down on the table.

I picked up the phone to call Suzanne. The line was dead. I dialed her number again and the line shut off. I waited fifteen minutes and tried it again. I tried over and over again. When I would dial the number it would automatically click off.

After trying the number six different times I called the operator. She tried the number for me, but she said that all of the phone services were out in that entire area because of the strong winds.

"Now this is really getting scary," I said to my husband as he walked into the kitchen. "All of the telephone services are out in Suzanne's area."

By 9:00 a.m. we decided we had waited long enough, so we loaded up the car and headed over to get our friends. This outrageous situation was just too daunting. We needed to bring them home where they could be safe.

Around noon we stopped for a hamburger in Burley and we filled up the car with gas. Darrell wanted to keep the tank filled because we had no idea what we might encounter once we reached the restricted area.

We arrived at the safe-haven stopping area at 12:57 p.m. We had made really good time getting there from Boise, but when they stopped us at the safety area they told us we couldn't go any farther.

The policeman explained, "I'm very sorry, but you will have to turn around and go back. We are not allowed to let anyone past this point, because the weather conditions are too unstable; in fact they are advising everyone that is still in the area to evacuate." He smiled and said, "You can turn around over there and then you will need to head back the way that you just came from. No one can enter the Tower County district."

I leaned my head down so that I could see the policeman standing outside the window and I said, "Thank you so much for your consideration, but that's why we are here. We have come to evacuate our friends and take them back to Boise with us."

"Well, the only time that they are letting anyone go in is after dark," he politely told me. "But the roads are a mess in the affected area; they are almost totally destroyed. A couple of more days of the disrupting windstorms and the highway will be completely gone, and you will no longer be able to tell where the highway had ever been."

The policemen looked away and let out a huge sigh, he seemed very distraught when he said, "I'm sorry, but I have lived in Tower County most of my life. I cannot believe that this has happened to my hometown and that now the town is almost gone. The heartless wind has never given up and I don't know how anyone will ever be able to stop it, because how do you stop the wind?"

He shook his head back and forth and told us, "It is some weird act of nature, because no one can tell what is causing the brutal winds in the first place." He rubbed his hand across his brow and told us, "I have sent my family to stay with my wife's mother in Idaho Falls. I just can't have them here in the middle of this situation, it is too unsettling. I have two twin girls and it is my job to keep them safe," He told us. "But I did get word here today that by last night everyone else in our neighborhood had been evacuated too."

"I am so sorry, I just can't believe that all of this is happening to your community," I responded back to the nice young man. "That's why we came all the way over here to get our friends. We just want to get our friends and take them back to Boise where they will be safe."

He then politely told us, "It is up to you if you want to wait here all day and try to find your friends when the National Guard goes through this evening that would be fine."

"The winds ease up at night so if you want to wait you will be able to go in after it gets dark." He added, "We had to let a few people go in last night so that they could help move their families out, but conditions have gotten so much worse today that no one is allowed to go in without security."

Darrell quickly answered, "Thank you that sounds great. Where would you like us to park? We don't want to be in anybody's way."

The policeman nodded as he answered, "Why don't you pull over by that guard rail. That will be out of the way if anyone needs to turn around. It is barely 1:00 p.m. right now, so it will be several hours before you can actually go through."

We parked where he had pointed to and we turned off the car. I looked at my watch. "Well it should be dark in about six hours, good thing we ate lunch in Burley and we brought plenty of water, coffee and a few snacks," I smugly remarked.

We got out of the car and stood in front of the hood for a few minutes looking towards the valley. We were still miles from where our friends lived, but the atmosphere look so strange off in the distance. It looked like one enormous dust cloud that engulfed everything for miles. It was uncanny. The whole region was taken over by some sort of monstrous smog cloud. The visibility was zero, it looked like everything in its path had been swallowed up and was just gone.

Every so often a black billowy cloud would burst into the air above the massive dust cloud and then everything would calm down again until the next black poof would appear. Being within a few miles of our friends was even scarier than when we talked with them on the phone. Seeing everything this close made it real and yet now we can't even communicate with them. It was so frightening because from here we could actually see that everything had just disappeared and the situation was much scarier than we had even imagined.

We could hear the howling of the gusty winds and it was haunting. It was much louder than just strong blowing winds; it was intensified to where you almost needed to cover your ears it was so powerful. The sound sent fear through my entire body. I had never heard anything so spine-chilling in my life. "No wonder the people of the community have been so afraid," I thought. "It doesn't even sound like blowing winds. It is more of a high moaning-type sound and it changes pitch as it blows in and out. It is absolutely terrifying." I rubbed my shoulders as I felt a cold shiver, and even standing in the warmth of the beautiful sunshine I felt cold.

I watched as one car after another came to the safe-haven point and turned around and went back. No one else chose to stay and wait all day.

As I stood there and stared towards the frightening valley Darrell reached into the trunk of the car and brought out two folding chairs for us to sit on. He realized that we were going to be there for awhile so we might as well get comfortable.

My husband got his binoculars out of the back seat and he started canvassing the area for things off in the distance. He wanted to see if he could find anything at all, any movement, any form of life; but as he searched he saw nothing, only miles upon miles of dust and nothingness.

When he got tired of looking through the binoculars he handed them to me and I also checked the surrounding area. Once again all I could see was the blinding dust storm; only this time it was magnified with the binoculars.

The sky was so blue and beautiful on this side of the safe-haven zone. It seemed impossible to think that there was so much devastation only a few miles on down the road. It was so serene and peaceful sitting here in our folding chairs, drinking coffee and eating cookies and just waiting for the time to pass.

Suddenly I saw something out of the corner of my eye. It was a long ways away. It was so far away that I wouldn't have noticed it without the binoculars. It looked like a giant black cloud rapidly moving across the atmosphere. But it was moving much faster than a normal cloud. I watched in amazement as the cloud raced across the sky and disappeared.

It went so fast that I didn't even have time to tell Darrell that I saw something.

I kept staring at the sky, but I couldn't spot the black cloud again. And Darrell had leaned back in his chair and was resting, so I didn't say anything to him about it.

I continued to search and search looking for the mysterious moving dark cloud, but it was gone. It had just vanished. It looked so out of place up against the flawless clear blue sky, but no matter how hard I searched I could not find it again.

All day long as we sat waiting for night to come I continued to keep watch, but the dark cloud never returned. The sky remained cloudless, clear and blue. I was very tired because I hadn't slept very well the night before and just sitting around doing nothing all day waiting for it to get dark was exhausting. Perhaps there really hadn't been a black cloud high up in the sky, maybe I had just imagined it from being so tired.

The sun felt so comforting and warm as we sat in the lawn chairs and waited, we couldn't have asked for a more perfect day. Darrell had dozed off and I decided to get comfortable and try to sleep in the chair for a few minutes too. I knew it was going to be a long night once we could finally get through the barricades. We were both sound asleep when we were awakened by the roar of the huge army vehicles.

The massive trucks roared into place as one by one they arrived at the safe-haven stopping area. There were at least thirty giant carriers loaded with clean up supplies, bulldozers and service men and women all dressed in army fatigues. We were in awe of the huge convoy. The lights on the enormous vehicles projected throughout the entire area. Each individual transport was as tall as a house and they were all equipped with heavy-duty artillery and they looked like they were preparing to go into a war zone.

When I was fully awake I realized that the howling winds had mysteriously stopped and it was finally dark out and it would soon be time to go. I studied the appearance of the National Guard soldiers and I wondered what they were preparing to find when they drove down into town. "They all looked so serious. Surely there was nothing in town that they would need to use their guns for," I thought. "Or had the army been told something different than we had been told?"

Darrell folded up the chairs and placed them in the trunk of the car so that we would be ready to leave when it was time to go. And then we stood quietly and observed as the people in charge prepared to take action.

We could tell by their cautious attitude that no one knew exactly what they were going to find when they arrived in the defective area. As we listened to the instructions a man came around and handed each one of us a heavy-duty army breathing mask. And then he instructed everyone on how to put it on.

The commander told the soldiers to break up into four separate units and they were to stay together in their unit. "Under no circumstances can anyone break off alone," the leader instructed everyone. "Look for any survivors and if you find anyone they are to be taken to the designated safety location." He went on, "Our job is to search for anyone that has been left behind and then to mark the property that has been checked out."

"Survivors, safety location?" I whispered to my husband. "What is going on here?"

"I don't know," he whispered shaking his head back and forth. "Just listen because they are treating us like we belong here and they are talking right in front of us. So, whatever they do we will just go along with them until we can find Suzanne and Gene and then we'll all get out of here."

I shook my head up and down that I understood, and I didn't say another word.

The person giving all of the instructions said, "Last night the state police along with a large unit from the Idaho National Guard started to evacuate a huge section of Tower County. They tried to get every person to leave the area, but some families refused to go and they had to be taken by force."

"Hopefully there will be no one left in any of the properties that we inspect." He continued, "The power has been off for several days and the water supply has been destroyed by all of the pollution from the blowing debris. The engineers have taken samples of the topsoil and they fear that the entire area has been contaminated. They worry about all of the spilled containers of paint, oil drums, chemicals and mixed pollutants that have been distributed into the ground."

The leader went on and said, "Many of the local people had gone to stay at the churches for safety. But all of the churches along with the jail, the schools and the hospital have all been emptied out. Everyone has been taken to the other side of Pocatello, Idaho Falls or to the safety location so hopefully the entire community should be vacated."

He sadly continued, "Today was the worst day that the area has experienced so far. Around noon today the wind gusts got so brutal that it uprooted a huge old oak tree over near the corner of Johnson and Myrtle Street near the center of town. The tree crushed a big gasoline tanker truck and the truck instantly burst into flames and started an uncontrollable fire. The fire was fanned by the horrific winds and it didn't stop until it reached the river."

He said, "The fire Department was not allowed to even try to contain the vicious firestorm because of the danger involved to the firefighters. Everything has become so dry because of the incessant daily winds and with the rapid speed of the firestorm and the severe winds that still continue to blow, the situations was just too treacherous. So, everyone was just forced to stand back and let it burn. There was absolutely nothing anyone could have done to stop it."

The speaker swallowed hard and put his head down before continuing on, "We have no idea of any lives lost in the fire because it happened before the evacuation could be completed. The evacuation was started last night, but it had carried on through most of the morning and the winds had started up again."

He continued, "The volunteers were trying desperately to get every person evacuated. But the whole evacuation had taken much longer than they had expected. They discovered that many people had been injured from all of the flying debris and downed trees. And they also had a number of people with severe breathing problems, and of course there were people who were already in poor health before the violent winds had even started and they all needed extra attention. So, of course it took them a lot longer than they had hoped."

The leader shook his head back and forth, "All we know for certain is that several of the volunteers were trapped in the enormous fire burst and they barely got out alive. One of the vehicles was trapped along with the volunteers and the people that they were transporting.

The fire, smoke and the horrendous winds made it impossible to complete the evacuation in the vehicle that they were originally in. Another military transport had to step in to help rescue the first vehicle and they got everyone to safety with only seconds to spare. They were forced to just abandon the first vehicle and within a few moments it was completely engulfed and destroyed in the fire"

"This has been a very desperate situation. Many of the people from the community got involved trying to help the injured people get out. It took every one of them helping each other to make the rescue effort a success. They said many of the young farmers and businessman just picked up the people that were trapped and carried them to safety on their shoulders. This is a very tight community. They are always there to help each other."

He somberly went on, "I have been told that the fire was so hot that it literally disintegrated everything in its path. It melted buildings, vehicles and buses...everything that got in its way."

"All of the buildings were closed up and they should have been deserted, but some of the business owners refused to leave. They didn't want to leave their businesses unattended because they were afraid of looters; and so many of them didn't leave until the very last minute. So, we must be prepared for anything tonight, we have no idea how bad the situation is until we get in there," he added.

"All that I know is that the volunteers that got out this morning have sent back word of how treacherous the situation is. They say that it is worse than any war zone that they have ever been in, because the enemy that we are fighting can not be defeated or controlled. The horrifying winds have a mind all their own and the wind has especially shown its power in the past few days by destroying everything that gets in its way." He added, "Be very cautious out there, do not let your guard down. Be aware of everything around you and be prepared to get to shelter as soon as the sun comes up."

Then the leader did something that took my husband and me by total surprise. He had the military chaplain come up in front of the group to lead the units in prayer before we headed off into town. I reached for Darrell's hand and squeezed it firmly, and then we bowed our heads and prayed with this amazing group of strangers.

When the prayer was done we looked at each other and shrugged our shoulders without saying a word. I had huge tears running down my face. We were both horrified by everything that we had heard from the leader; we had no idea what was going on.

After watching the dust through the binoculars all afternoon we knew that we had gotten ourselves into a terrible mess. We had never planned to, we had just come over to get our friends and take them back to Boise where they could be safe. But after listening to everything that has been going on over here we realized this was going to be a lot more difficult than we first thought it would be.

The commander was finished talking and he asked if there were any questions. Apparently everyone else had been highly briefed on the situation and they knew exactly what they were to do. Because there were no questions everyone instantly put on their breathing devices and within a few minutes the soldiers had returned to their places in the trucks. The police removed all of the barricades and we could now move forward into the valley.

FOURTEEN

Tower County

W e quickly got into our car and fell into place behind the third large transport vehicle. We proceeded right along as if we were part of the group. At first it was a little intimidating to be wedged between two huge army movers, but within a few miles we were grateful for the extra protection.

As we came around the canyon wall and began to drop down into the valley we observed a sight that was scarier than any words could ever express. I gasped and held my breath for several seconds as I sat forward in the seat and gazed out the front window at the odd colored smog environment that encompassed the entire region.

The air was so dense that there were huge globs of dirt that would kind of dance up throughout the gloomy surroundings and then just kind of float off into space. The heavy air looked like it could actually hold a person up if the person were to relax and lean back and just drift away.

It was so hot and the stagnant atmosphere looked so thick and vile that we could tell that the air down in the valley had been totally polluted. We could easily see why the engineers felt that the entire area was contaminated, because it looked like we were driving through a junky swamp land that had not been inhabited for a long time. It gave you such a feeling of claustrophobia; everything around us was so oppressed and lifeless. I found it hard to remember to breathe. In fact I'm sure that we would not have been able to breathe at all without the army breathing devices.

We stared out the car window in disbelief because it was so eerie it looked like something out of a horror movie set. Between the slow moving haze and the unsettled floating dust you almost expected giant dinosaurs to appear out of the fog at anytime.

The convoy moved along at a snail's pace trying to figure out the direction of the highway. The roadway was so totally covered with dirt and filth that it made it completely indistinguishable. As we drove through the thick dusty fog, the heavy refuse on the road parted and lightly blew up into the air as we attempted to crawl along trying to follow the highway.

There were no winds, so the air was exceptionally compressed and dry from several days of constant wind gusts and blustery weather. The face masks were bulky and cumbersome, but I don't think we could have survived without them because the air was so tainted. No wonder the policeman at the safe-haven zone had been so distraught about his community. I would have sent my family away too. In fact, I wouldn't have believed all of this if I hadn't seen it with my own eyes.

I then thought about the many local people who did not have the special heavy-duty breathing devices, how did they survive?

The roads were cluttered with downed trees, road signs, telephone and power poles, stalled cars and huge tumbleweeds piled everywhere. There were long boards with nails poking out that looked like they had just been ripped out of someone's wall. There was wiring and housing insulation and large pieces of cupboards and shelving.

We saw roof shingles, crumbled up house siding and broken glass from ruined windows. There were large patches of wall plaster, entire billboards, patio furniture and sizeable sections of fencing. And the soot on the highway was so deep that you could hardly tell where the pavement started and where it dropped off.

"This is a main highway," I had to remind myself. Yet it looked like something out of a ghost town. The electricity had been out for a few days and so there were no street lights and every structure along the way had been evacuated and looked condemned. Most of the buildings had lost their windows and a large portion of their roofs. Many of the walls were caved in and when the headlights of the vehicles shown on the structures you could see all the way through to the backside of the building.

Parked cars were covered with fallen tree branches, weeds, overturned trash barrels, road symbols and speed limit signs that were still attached to their post. Several cars had large patches of paint removed after being sandblasted by sand and flying dirt and rocks. It was even hard to distinguish what color many of the vehicles were supposed to be, they all looked the same when they were covered in grime.

Although, we had been on this road many times before it looked so different that we were unable to get our bearings to know exactly where we were. It was hard to tell where the turn off was to our friend's property. We weren't sure if we would recognize it with all of the cluttered mess because there were none of the usual markings that told us where to turn.

Suddenly the lead truck signaled that he was turning right on the first road up ahead. As he turned, every vehicle behind him from unit one turned and followed him, including us. The second group drove on to the next road and then turned left. The third unit continued straight on down the highway and so did the fourth unit.

Our group drove down the gravel road until we came to the first farmhouse on the left side of the street. We had seven huge military vehicles in our unit. Every one of the soldiers got out and started to search through what remained of the destroyed old farmhouse. A huge tree had been uprooted and its enormous branches engulfed the entire old house splitting the house right down the middle.

Darrell and I stood quietly outside of our car and watched the soldiers check the entire property; they motioned that they had found no one. Apparently this family had already been evacuated. The all-clear signal was given and a large yellow X was sprayed across the front yard to show that it had been inspected and no one was left behind. Within seconds all of the soldiers were loaded up and we moved on to the next farmhouse.

We followed along with the army convoy and we watched as they stopped at each farmhouse and checked it out for survivors and then marked the front yard with a large yellow X. Then each soldier got back into the military trucks and moved on to the next property. House after house, street after street they checked, but the whole area was deserted.

Then we came to a large building that looked like it might have been a junior high or high school. Most of the windows were blown out, the power had been gone for several days and it was dark, and there was trash scattered everywhere so it was very hard to identify. The building looked like it had been empty for a long time, but it probably hadn't.

Every one of the soldiers gathered around as the lead driver hollered out instructions. He told them, "Be very careful and thoroughly check every single room, every closet and every cupboard. Last night the police found five young children hiding in one of the broom closets down at the grade school. Apparently the kids had been there for four days. They were huddled together afraid to go anywhere because of the violent winds."

"The closet was right next door to the restroom, so they could use the restroom and then run back into the closet to hide. When the winds would die down at night they would take a flashlight that they had found in the janitors closet and go to the cafeteria for food and bottled water and then they would go right back into the closet, because they felt safe inside the closet," he told them.

The lead driver went on, "The parents had been taken to Pocatello and they had been told that all of the children from the school had been taken to the safety location. The parents didn't know until the police discovered the five kids last night that they weren't with all of the other school children."

"When they evacuated all of the other kids at the school four days ago, those five kids ran and hid in the closet because they were so afraid. So be very careful and check every corner we don't want anyone left behind," he said. "This is a high school so the students might hide anywhere."

After checking the premises thoroughly the soldiers marked the front of the school parking lot with a large yellow X and then everyone got back into the military movers and we were off. This was the largest inspection that the soldiers had done so far. It had taken them several hours to thoroughly go through the entire school. Even though we had to wait for them we were so impressed by their competence. They had a job to get done and they did not stop until they were certain there was no one in the building.

When we were back in our own car I said to my husband, "It seems odd that we wouldn't see at least one person or one vehicle trying to drive around. It is so strange because everyone is just gone."

"I know," he replied. "I was thinking that myself."

Our unit had driven up and down one street after another until every house that we could find was checked for survivors. We finally turned on Gallop Lane and I recognized the name of the street. "This is Suzanne and Gene's lane," I excitedly told my husband. "Their farm is the third property from the highway and it set back off of the road. It is down a short lane on the east side of the street."

"Yes, this is their street," my husband acknowledged. "But nothing looks very familiar; we are going to have to look really close to figure out which house is theirs."

We counted and watched as properties one and two were checked out and marked. When the convoy came to the third farmhouse, the property of our friends, I had to cover my face to keep from screaming; because half of the house was flattened, and the yard was cluttered and destroyed by the four huge fallen trees.

We might not have been able to recognize our friend's property at all because of all the damage, but we saw their white Toyota parked out near where the front door used to be. We had been with them when they bought the car; it had been brand new three years ago.

I was absolutely trembling. I feared that they would find the bodies of our good friends buried in the wreckage in their basement. Because that is where Suzanne had told me they would be hiding when we talked on the phone last night. "Last night," I repeated in my head. "It had only been last night since I had talked to her." So much had happened today it was hard to comprehend that it had only been 24 hours since we talked.

When the soldiers gave the all-clear signal that they had found no one in the house I almost screamed out loud. I let out a huge sigh of relief and bowed my head in thanks to the Lord. This whole situation made me absolutely ill.

"Well, it is a relief that they are not here, but where do you think they are?" I asked my husband. "At least they were not buried in the basement crawl-space because that is where she told me they would be hiding."

My husband answered, "They must have been evacuated and placed in the safety location wherever that is."

Their property was marked with a yellow X and all of the soldiers were loaded back up and ready to move on to the next farmhouse. Property after property they inspected and marked every house, but we found no one.

My husband and I thought about breaking away and heading back to the safe-haven zone, but we weren't sure that we could find it. Although, we had successfully discovered our friends property, we had not yet rescued them like we had planned to do and we were afraid to break away and try to get out on our own.

In fact the thought of driving around in this shattered war zone by ourselves was beyond frightening. We decided to remain with the convoy and we would follow them wherever they went. We knew that we would be safer staying with the military trucks than we would be wandering around on our own.

After finishing up the entire section our unit headed towards the center of town to meet up with the other military units. We had checked every house for survivors and found no one; and they marked every house that they inspected with the yellow X. Apparently we had completed our assignment and were ready to head back.

The other military units were waiting for us where the fire had taken place earlier in the day. As we approached the fire zone district we could not believe what we saw. It looked like it was daylight because the entire section glowed with orange-hot coals left over from the fire. The glowing embers gave the smog an auburn glazed appearance that continued to float throughout the entire burned area

Everything was burned and destroyed. Every house, every small business, the whole region was blackened beyond recognition. Only the leftover glowing-hot embers were all that remained.

"The smoke from the fire must have been the huge black puffs that we could see earlier today when we were up in the safe-haven location," I told my husband. "As I watched the gusty smog hovering down in the valley I could see a puff of black smoke every so often. That must have been when the fire was at its worst."

As the soldiers checked out the fire zone, we stood by and waited for them to finish up. We had no idea where we were going next. We stood by the car and watched the men in uniform solemnly walk around the outskirts of the burned fire district and pace back and forth.

All of a sudden I felt a soft breeze blowing my hair into my face and I felt a strange chill go up my spine. I looked at my watch and it was 5:40 in the morning. It would soon be daylight and the dreadful winds would return to claim the rest of its victims.

I watched the men in the military units to see how they would respond to the breeze, but I could tell by watching them that they were not even thinking about morning. They were concentrating on the dreadful fire and for now they had forgotten all about the wind.

We were standing probably half a block away from where the soldiers were studying the charred remains. And we could tell that when the wind started to blow they never even looked up because they were busy checking out all of the horrendous damage from the firestorm. They were completely focused on the overwhelming destruction. It was an unbelievable sight unlike anything any of us had ever seen before.

There was so much devastation and everything was a total loss. As we stood back and watched the military inspect the fire damage we were frightened by the ghostlike appearance that the soldiers gave off as they walked around. Between the goopy smog and the eerie silence the entire area looked like an old London graveyard where the Frankenstein monster would soon come shuffling through the middle of everyone.

It was a very haunting situation for all of us to experience. Many of the soldiers were trying to hold their emotions together by rubbing their eyes with their fingers and wiping their hands across their face. The sight of so much obliteration was just too overpowering to comprehend.

No one was paying any attention to what time it was. The entire situation that we were dealing with was so abnormal that it was difficult to concentrate. Most of them had completely forgotten about the wind. They forgot that the winds could change and would come to life when it got to be daylight. Just seeing the mammoth fire was so disturbing, it was almost hypnotic because it was so massive and destructive it seemed unreal.

But I knew that the wind wouldn't wait for anyone. First it was just a slight breeze and within a few minutes the gusts began throwing dirt, sparks and ashes everywhere.

Suddenly the lead driver realized that the wind had come up and we had stayed longer than he had planned. He began to shout out commands for everyone to return to their vehicles then he too raced towards the first military truck. Immediately everyone got back into their trucks and prepared to leave. Each huge vehicle thundered to life and we slowly began to crawl back through the streets the exact way that we had just come.

As we bounced back through the cluttered streets the wind got stronger and stronger and within minutes it felt like it had reached hurricane strength. Each gust would kind of pull you in and then thrust you out and then immediately it would propel you back another direction. Over and over and over again we could feel the strength of the merciless gusts push and pull and then just release us and kind of throw us away.

It was absolutely terrifying being in the center of this mindless enemy. As we were driving through the core of the storm we were able to observe the wind change and we could feel it get stronger within seconds; we could visibly see it grow angrier every minute until it had reached its terrifying force.

We feared for our lives and I would have never believed this monstrosity if we hadn't been placed directly in the heart of its rage. We had been able to visibly watch it construct as it first started out as a slight breeze and then just get worse until it was a gigantic monster that had completely lost all control. Now there were huge branches, papers,

95

trash and signs haphazardly whirling up and down the street in every direction.

The garbage would smash into the side of our car and continue to blow on down the street thrashing into anything in its way. We watched in horror as flying debris narrowly whipped past our windshield and then blew chaotically at all of the soldiers riding in the back of the huge open transport trucks. They ducked and dodged trying fervently to keep from getting smacked up the side of the head with a swirling branch or a window awning.

You could just sense the panic in the driver of the front vehicle because he began going faster trying to escape the inevitable destruction of the wind. I'm sure that he was remembering all of the volunteers that had gotten caught up in the winds from yesterday after staying out in the open for too long. He continued to pick up speed until the convoy was traveling much faster than it should have been moving.

Darrell and I were absolutely horrified by all of the flying signs, clutter and trash. It was surprising how swiftly the wind had become so violent. The dust flew and scattered as we raced along the highway trying to trace our pathway back to the way that we had come.

Our visibility in the car was absolutely zero. It was all my husband could do to follow the huge transport truck in front of us and try to go fast enough to keep the massive truck behind us from running us down. The winds had become so severe that we could not see anything around us; Darrell had to totally depend on the army trucks for direction. I had no idea if their visibility was better than ours or not, but I sure hoped that it was because we could not see anything.

Without warning the lead truck abruptly turned off of the highway and headed across the dessert on an old abandoned dirt road. He was rapidly throwing rocks, dirt and sand up in our face from every direction as he hurriedly roared across the desert up towards the steep mountainside. Our car spun and slid over the dusty dirt road trying desperately to keep pace with all of the giant army vehicles. I held my breath as we almost turned completely around in a circle.

"Where are we going?" I screamed grabbing the dash board as we bounced across the pitted old road. "Why are we heading for the dessert? Isn't this where all of the wind storms are coming from?" I screamed at the top of my lungs.

My husband didn't answer he just shook his head and tried to keep up with the powerful huge army trucks. Our poor Chrysler 300 was not made to race through the dessert. It was too close to the ground. It bounced and jumped and swerved and almost rolled.

Finally, the huge truck that we had been following slowed down as we approached a giant cave-like gravel pit located in the side of the mountain. As we entered into the massive cave everything instantly calmed down. The winds were gone and all of the trucks slowed down to a crawl as the lead driver continued on until he had traveled deep into the base of the cavern. We cautiously followed along behind him until we were so far inside of the mountain that we could no longer see the front entrance of the cave.

The cavern was vast and it was huge enough to easily hold ten times the number of military vehicles that we had in our party. One by one every truck in all four units pulled inside the cavern and neatly parked and turned off their engines. It was dark and eerie, but at least we had escaped the violent winds.

Every soldier got out of their trucks and removed their breathing devices and put them in the back of a large trailer to be sanitized. We followed suit and we each placed our mask in the trailer too. Apparently none of us would need them any longer.

We had no idea where we were or what we were supposed to do now. No one talked to us or gave us any instructions, but everyone else acted as if they knew exactly where they were and what they were supposed to be doing. Each one of them walked over to the steep railing that surrounded the cavern and they began climbing down the side of the cave on long metal spiral ladders.

There were several ladders and it appeared that this was the only way to get down to wherever they needed to go. We could hear the clanging of their military boots and the chatter of their voices as they swiftly scurried down the long sturdy ladders and disappeared.

One by one every soldier climbed down until we were the only people left at the top of the cavern. Looking over the side we could see that each soldier had climbed deep inside of the earth until every one of them had reached the bottom and had somehow vanished into the shadowy unknown.

As we stood on the top of the cavern and looked down into the deep abyss we realized that the massive cavern where we were standing had become completely silent. Every one of the soldiers had disappeared and we could once again hear the distant howling of the senseless winds far off towards the entrance of the cave. We had no desire to return to the way that we had just come in, so we knew we had no other choice but to follow the rest of our associates down into the dark frightening unknown.

FIFTEEN

The Cavern

I looked at my husband and said, "Well, are you ready? We really don't have a choice except to follow the soldiers. I sure don't want to stay up here alone and I'm not going back out to face the wind so it looks like the only way to go is down."

My husband smirked at me as he started down the steep metal stairway ahead of me. I grimaced as I started down the long spiral staircase holding tightly to the railing. Down, down, down we went, around and around we continued downward as our feet clanged against the rungs of the stairway as we made our way closer to the bottom of the ladder with each step we took.

The metal spiral staircase was long, but it was solid and fairly easy to climb down, and it was securely bolted to the sides of the mountain. The walls were solid rock behind the metal ladders and they smelled musty and damp like wet dirt, but there were small safety lights scattered throughout the cave so that the cavern was not completely dark. For some reason it appeared that this huge cavern was set up to be used in case of an emergency; because the ladders and lights were well-maintained.

We could not descend the stairs as quickly as the trained soldiers, but we kept up a steady pace until we had climbed all the way to the bottom; deep inside of the mountain.

When we reached the bottom of the cavern we found a large platform section with several open doorways that led out to a wide type of earthen hallway that seemed to go all of the way around the cavern.

All of the soldiers had disappeared to their designated areas and there were no people around for us to ask directions. We cautiously started walking down the hallway until we came to an open doorway that led into room with two large windows. The windows allowed us to see down into an enormous laboratory. The laboratory was filled with people dressed in blue lab clothes. Everyone was dressed the same, in clean, crisp blue uniform style jumpsuits.

We stood at the windows and watched all of the people in the lab for several minutes. Not one person noticed us watching them because they were all busy taking notes and studying a giant surround computer type screen. The screen encircled the entire room and it went from ceiling to floor and every person from any location could watch whatever was on the screen.

From where we were standing we could clearly see that they were watching the violent wind movement that was going on outside of the cavern. It was daylight outside now so the visibility was much clearer than it had been in the darkness the night before.

We could see garbage flying around and large masses of dust and dirt slamming through the air. Hefty tree branches would split apart and be launched up into the sky until they were completely out of sight. The stressed branches had been fighting the winds for many days, but they just couldn't hold onto the trees any longer.

Signs would shoot across the highway and crash into the side of some building and then smash into tiny splinters. Huge road signs would let go after several days of the hammering winds and they would gyrate straight up in the air and never return.

It was much easier to watch the wind destruction when you were watching it from inside a laboratory than when you are out in the center of the ferocious winds. When you are out in the wind you cannot see anything.

My husband and I stood their mesmerized by the pictures on the screens. The powerful cameras spanned the area and you could see the extensive destruction that had been caused by the violent windstorms. The cameras divided some of the pictures into sections and the scientists were able to watch many areas at the same time. It appeared that they could see for miles in every direction.

Suddenly the cameras focused on the giant wind turbines that were located out in Tower County. We could not hear what was being said about the turbines, but as we watched we could tell that the blades were rapidly spinning much, much faster than a normal wind turbine. They were twirling so quickly that you could barely see the blades as they swiftly spun out of control. They looked like they would fly apart at any time.

The large turbines were absolutely hypnotic as they took on a life of their own. As I concentrated on the gigantic wind machines they actually looked like they were beginning to move. I trembled as I watched the monstrous machines begin to saunter back and forth trying to break away from their mountings and poles. "They're alive," I whispered to my husband. "What should we do?" I was absolutely traumatized as I stared at the wind turbines on the big computer screen.

"What's alive?" My husband answered as he stared down at the people in the laboratory.

I tightly closed my eyes trying to block out the frightening images that were performing across the screens. I kept my eyes closed for several seconds and when I opened them again the wind turbines were just wind turbines. They were spinning out of control, but I could tell that they weren't really walking. I let out a big sigh of relief when I figured out that I had just been imagining things; the turbines had just looked like they were alive.

As I closely stared at the giant computer screen I began to relax and I realized how beautiful the skies were directly behind the fast moving wind turbines. The sky was clear and beautiful, it was unmistakably flawless. As I watched the turbines swiftly rotate around and around I blinked because I once again saw the rapidly moving black clouds float across the sky and abruptly disappear. The dark cloud looked just like the cloud that I had seen at the safe-haven position when we first arrived. "Did you see that?" I asked my husband. "That black cloud racing through the sky and then just disappearing?"

"No, I'm sorry, I was watching that scientist working with the giant chalkboard," he replied. "I was trying to figure out what he was writing. He was watching the screen showing the wind turbines and then he promptly started scribbling notes about what he observed. But it is a little too far away for me to read it," my husband added.

"Are you lost?" a strong voice spoke up from behind us.

I jumped as I quickly turned around to see a tall man in one of the blue lab jumpsuits. "Yes, I guess we are," I stated.

"What are you doing over here on the military side," the man politely asked us.

"Oh is that why we had to climb down a long spiral ladder?" my husband amusingly responded.

The tall man started laughing, "You came in down the metal ladders? How did you get to the back side of the facility?" He then reached out his hand and introduced himself, "I am sorry to be so rude, my name is Dr. Benjamin Keyes and I am the lead meteorological scientist for the wind project here in Tower County."

My husband and I both introduced ourselves and then I told him, "We went into the restricted area with the military convey in search of our friends. We were trying to rescue them and take them back to Boise with us. We found their property, but we never found them. So, we remained with the convoy and they drove in through the military entrance and we just followed them."

The doctor nodded his head up and down that he understood and then he got more serious and he said, "I was called in several days ago along with my staff from Penn State to set up a scientific wind study because of the abnormal weather problems that are happening here in this valley. This whole situation is unbelievable. I have never seen anything quite like it before. We have been working on this for six days and we aren't any closer to a solution than we were when we started. Nothing adds up. Usually after two days we have figured out all of the strange weather problems and we can answer most of the questions that we have been sent to answer. But this situation is different it is unlike anything we have ever dealt with in the past."

"Where exactly are we?" I innocently asked Dr. Keyes. "We were just following the military units and we ended up here, but where is here?"

"This is a large military emergency safety location. It is just one of many massive caverns across the United States that can be immediately used to set up as an emergency facility," the doctor explained. "The caverns are all equipped with lighting, heavy duty power use or back up generators. They also have the capabilities to set up massive computer screens like the one that you were watching a few minutes ago."

He continued, "The cavern has an emergency hospital and morgue facility and a huge living area if needed; large enough to house probably 30,000 people if they wanted to stay here." He continued, "I have worked in several facilities just like this one all across the United States. The facilities have an emergency food and clean water supply and they have the capabilities to house many families for up to several weeks at a time."

He went on, "They are also used for military training and military field housing. Actually in this situation many of the people that have come here were only brought in because of an emergency situation and they needed somewhere close to come when they were evacuated."

He said, "I understand that some of the other people were taken to Pocatello or Idaho Falls or one of the other surrounding towns. If they had time to plan to evacuate, many of them went to stay with relatives that were not too far away, but were out of the vicinity of the wind storms. They didn't all come here to the compound."

"Many of the caverns that are like this one are maintained on a continual basis because they know that they will be needed several times throughout the year. They are kept ready with a handful of fulltime workers maintaining them at all times." He told us, "Those are the easiest laboratories to work in because we can just walk in and everything is already set up the way that we want it to be."

"The caverns are set up for natural disasters like storms, floods, or in case of a terrorist attack. The government uses the massive caves as safety locations because they are obviously stable and they are located up in higher ground in the side of a mountain.

There are many hidden caverns just like this one within a short distance of almost every big city in the United States. Most people do not even know that they exist. Many of the old dirt roads that you see shooting off into the desert are actually huge safety location caverns and if you were to travel to the inside you would discover a massive facility just like this one." Dr. Keyes exclaimed, "This cavern is one of the nicest safety locations that I have been in and it has not been used very often."

"I never knew that there were laboratories set up in the side of the mountains," I said, "That is amazing. Now we will be looking for caverns every time we travel."

We all paused for a few seconds and returned our thoughts to the giant screens that were all around the laboratory. Dr. Keyes interrupted our thoughts and he said, "When I first walked up and you guys were looking at the screens you were saying something about a fast moving black cloud." He asked me, "We haven't noticed any black clouds, where did you think you saw it?"

"Actually, I have seen it twice," I told him. "The first time that I saw it was when we were stopped out at the safe-haven zone." I added, "The sky was clear and beautiful and that's why I noticed the black cloud in the first place, because it was so out of place up next to the flawless sky. The fast moving cloud just kind of came out of nowhere and then it rapidly disappeared and I couldn't find it again in the binoculars."

Then I told him, "But to be honest with you I haven't had a lot of sleep the past few days and I could easily be imaging things. It was moving much faster than any cloud that I have ever seen before. I really don't think that a cloud could move that fast."

"But you thought you just saw the same thing again a few minutes ago on the big screen in this laboratory?" he questioned.

"I don't know," I told him, "It looked the same to me, but the first time that I saw it I tried to convince myself that there really hadn't been anything there since I couldn't find it again." I shook my head back and forth, "And to tell you the truth it moves so fast I'm not sure exactly what it could be."

Dr. Keyes walked over to a small metal box that was built into the side of the wall and he keyed in several numbers to release a microphone. He took the microphone out of the box and spoke to one of the attendants that were working on the computers screens down in the lab in front of us.

When the attendant answered the phone he turned around and looked up to where Dr. Keyes was standing next to us and he motioned that he could understand him. Dr. Keyes then said to the attendant, "I want you to slow screen the pictures that were taken out at the wind farm about fifteen minutes ago. Break them down into 5 second intervals, so that you can stop the screen when I ask you to."

It was amazing to watch as the screens came to life in slow motion, frame by frame until it came to the place where I had seen the rapid moving black cloud.

"There," I said, "Directly behind the second wind turbine on the right."

Dr. Keyes talked into the microphone, "Hold that frame and magnify it until it is recognizable. There is definitely something there, but it is so minute it is hard to tell what it is."

The attendant enlarged the picture many times as every scientist in the lab studied the screen and took notes. As they enlarged the black cloud on the screen it was evident that the black mass was not a cloud. It was actually made up of millions of tiny moving parts. It all meshed together so that it looked like one single mass from far away, but when it was enlarged you could tell that it was actually millions of individual moving pieces.

As we watched the giant screen we had no idea what we were looking at, but when we turned back to look at the doctor he got a strange look on his face and he abruptly said to the attendant in the microphone, "I will be right down." Then Dr. Keyes turned to us and apologized and said, "I'm sorry, but I really need to go."

He told us, "If you follow the hall all the way around to the left you will come into the reception area and they will give you a designated room to stay in while you are here at the facility." Then he politely stated, "It was nice meeting both you." And then he closed the microphone box and he was gone.

Darrell and I looked at each other and I shrugged my shoulders and I said, "What do you think that was all about?"

"I have no idea," my husband answered with a puzzled look on his face. "But we'll go and find the reception area as the doctor suggested because it looks like we have to stay here for awhile." We headed down the dirt hallway and we never once met another person until we reached the end of the hall and we came into a small office location. As we turned the corner we came into a neatly organized reception area. A young man in a military uniform was sitting behind a huge desk and he asked us what we needed.

I smiled as I talked to the young man, "Dr. Keyes told us to come down here to find a place for us to stay while we are here."

The proper young soldier handed me a paper to fill out with all of our information on it; our name, phone number, and address. After we were done filling everything out he handed us two sets of navy blue sweats to wear later on when we needed a change of clothes, then he led us down the hall to a big crowded room.

The room was a huge open space and it was filled with a lot of people. There were people of all ages and they were sitting around on comfortable looking chairs and couches and just kind of waiting and visiting with each other. There were several small groups of children and they were playing puzzles and games at a big table on the far side of the room. We had no idea what everyone was waiting for, but they all appeared to be waiting for something.

We didn't talk with anyone and no one attempted to talk to us. Several people looked up as we walked by, but soon they went back to doing whatever they had been doing before we came. They went on talking to each other as if we weren't even there.

We left the area where all of the people were sitting and the young man led us down the hall past rooms that appeared to be designated as living quarters. It was a long narrow hallway and every door to every room was closed as we walked by and the rooms seemed empty. We never saw any other people in the hallway and there was no one coming out of any of the rooms as we passed by.

It was an extremely long hall and we passed probably over a hundred rooms until we finally arrived at the very end of the hallway. There were no other rooms beyond that area and our room was the last room on the left. It was a little bit spooky being so far away from everyone else and to be the very last room on the end of the hall. I looked back down the hall from where we had just come from and looked like it was at least a mile away.

This was not like staying at a Best Western or the Marriott. We didn't have a lot that we could say about what room we stayed in. It was creepy enough just knowing that we were staying inside of a cave and there were no windows or doors to the outside. The walls were finished, so it looked like a real building, but we had to constantly remind ourselves that we were inside of a mammoth cavern.

It was very dark in the hallway and I was almost afraid to have the soldier leave, because I knew that once he left we would be completely alone. But it was not like we could just ask for another room closer to the other people. This is where we had been appointed, so this is where we needed to stay.

When the soldier opened the door to our room we were quite surprised at how nice it was. It was very small with two bunk beds and a sink, but it was neat and clean. "This is where you will be staying while you are here at the military safety location," he said. "Your room number is 1247. The doors do not have locks, so you do not need a key."

"Oh great," I said to myself as I thought about being clear down on the very end of the hallway with no one else around. "There are no locks on the doors so we can't even lock ourselves inside of our room."

The nice young soldier told us, "The community showers and bathroom facilities are located down the hall on the left. Every shower facility has clean towels and wash cloths and the small cupboard under the sink will have shampoo, soap and any of the other items you might need. There is a hamper to place your towel and washcloths in when you are finished."

"The cafeteria is located back down the hall the way that you came in. It is the big room off to the right," the young man told us. "All of the food is provided by an emergency government fund to help people stranded in a situation like this one. They have declared all of Tower County as an emergency disaster area by the government and that is why this military safety location has been put into use."

He then nodded his head up and down, "If you need anything just come back to the reception area and there will always be someone there 24 hours a day." He started to leave then he turned back around and said, "Also, there is no phone reception inside the cavern so you will not be able to reach anyone from the outside." He continued, "The phone service has been down in this area for several days so you probably couldn't call out anyway, but I thought I would just let you know."

"That's a little scary," I thought to myself as the young man turned around to leave. "Thank you," I politely said to the soldier as he started off down the hall. After he left we realized that we were starved. We hadn't eaten much of anything since we had that hamburger in Burley the day before. We had cookies and some snacks while we were waiting at the safe-haven zone, but that was yesterday. It was time for us to find the cafeteria to get something to eat.

We stopped in the restroom and then we walked back in the direction that the young man had told us to go. The cafeteria was bright and cheerful with hundreds of round tables and chairs and the room was filled with lots of people. There were several families sitting around eating. It was a regular cafeteria style with trays and a rail to slide your tray on as you went along. You then chose your food from the server that stood behind the glass.

All of the food looked delicious and I couldn't believe how hungry I was. I got a chicken dinner with mashed potatoes and gravy, green beans and a roll. I chose a small coffee and a carton of milk to drink. The food was hot and everything looked clean and fresh.

Darrell got the halibut and chips dinner, with coffee and water to drink. He was very impressed with the three large portions of halibut that they placed on his plate. He had French fries and a bowl of mixed vegetables and a hot roll.

We carried our trays over to the first available chairs and sat down to enjoy our...I guess lunch. I looked at my watch for the first time in hours and discovered that it was 11:14 a.m. I felt disoriented because so much had been going on since our arrival that we had lost all track of time.

After we finished eating we sat at the table and had a second cup of coffee. As I looked around the room I noticed that everyone in the room was dressed alike. They all had the dark blue sweatpants and a dark blue sweatshirt like the receptionist had given us.

There were entire families dressed just the same. Many of the small children had oversized sweatshirts that hung down to their knees, but they weren't complaining. Even the smallest children seemed to be thankful to be safely inside of the cave.

We were so pleased with our lunch and the food was even better than we had expected. My chicken was fried to perfection and they used real potatoes for their mashed potatoes. Darrell said his fish was wonderful. It was fresh and crunchy and he really liked the French fries.

We were finished with lunch so we decided to walk around and take a look at the rest of the facility. As we walked back into the large waiting room where all of the people had been before we discovered that many of the people were gone. Most of the couches and chairs were empty. There was hardly anyone left inside of the giant room.

"Where have all of the people gone to?" I ask my husband as we apprehensively walked through the large room. "This place was packed only a few minutes ago."

"I don't know," my husband answered as surprised as I was. "Maybe they have all gone back to their rooms."

We walked out to the reception desk where the young man had been before and for some strange reason, he was gone too. And the desk was empty.

We headed for the doorway straight ahead and turned to the left to go down the hallway in a direction that we had never been down before. This hallway had individual rooms just like the hallway where our room was and like our hallway this hall was empty too. There were no signs of any people anywhere and the hall was completely silent. We stood perfectly still listening, but there no sound at all.

Then way at the very end of the hall we spotted someone sitting in a chair. The person's head was down and he was leaned forward. Slowly and cautiously we crept towards the person with his head down, but he never looked up. We passed room after room as we walked towards the man, but no one came out of any of the doors. When we got to the end of the hallway we saw that the man was not sitting in a chair, but he was sitting in a wheelchair. He was slumped over frontward and he appeared to be asleep. As I got closer I could see that his hands and body were strapped to the wheelchair as if someone was afraid that he would fall out and get hurt if he was not strapped in.

I quietly walked over to the side of the chair and stood there looking down at the man. He woke up with a start and he began to scream, "No, no, no," he shouted. "Get them away, get them away," he squealed, "They are all over me, help me, help me, help me," the man shouted as he then lifted his head and looked up towards me.

I had to jump back to keep from screaming myself, because the man's face was so appalling. He was mutilated beyond recognition. He was covered in some kind of insect bites. His hands were eaten clear to the muscle and you could see his bones poking out from the skin. His ears were gone and he had huge chunks removed from his neck and his jaw. His eyes were totally swollen shut and he acted as if he was permanently blind. I felt like I was going to pass out, because the sight of this man was so grotesque. I felt so sorry for him. Something had absolutely devoured his flesh and somehow he had survived; if you want to call it surviving.

As the poor man continued to scream a lady in one of the blue lab suits came running down the hall and pushed me aside. "You are not supposed to be down here," she looked at me and shouted. "Stay away from him," she screamed as she pushed the man's wheelchair down the hall and into a private room.

My husband and I just stood there and stared as the lady disappeared inside one of the rooms with the man still screaming. "What is going on here?" I quietly whispered to my husband.

"I don't know, but I think we should find Suzanne and Gene and get out of this place," he exclaimed. "This whole situation is crazy. First the winds, then the smog, then the fire, then this cavern with a giant laboratory, then some black moving cloud that everyone gets so excited about and now a man that is half-eaten alive. What next; spaceships?" He then admitted, "I am so exhausted, I don't think I can take any more of these strange surprises."

"Me either, let's just find our way back to our room and rest for awhile," I told him. "I think we will feel better if we sleep."

As we walked past the door where the lady in the blue jumpsuit had taken the screaming man we read the sign on the door that said...Private Area Keep Out. Then we slowly walked back in the direction that we had previously come from. When we reached the reception desk we noticed the young man that had led us to our room and he was once again sitting behind the desk. He smiled and nodded his head to us as we went by.

When we walked into the large waiting room with all of the couches and chairs the room was again packed with people sitting in every chair. There were a lot of people just talking and waiting just as they were before. Every person was wearing the same dark navy blue sweatpants and sweatshirts.

"That would be an easy type of outfit that would fit all types of people...men, women and even children; and most of these people came here with absolutely nothing," I thought. "So, sweatpants and sweatshirts would be ideal for everyone as a complete outfit."

After walking past all of the people we started to our room. Both of us were just wiped out. It had been a very exhausting day.

114

We again walked to the very end of the hallway until we reached our room 1247 and then we walked in. "We will be safe here," I thought to myself as I closed the door. "It will feel good to sleep and we have nowhere that we need to go and absolutely nothing that we need to be doing. We can check on our friends later, but for now we can rest." I chose the top bunk and my husband sprawled out on the lower bunk. Within a few seconds I could hear him lightly snoring, he was so tired. It had been an interesting past 24 hours.

I turned off the main light and an automatic night light stayed on softly glowing over by the door. I climbed up on my bunk to go to sleep. As I lay on my bunk trying to fall asleep I noticed how nice and clean the small room was. The walls were white plaster, just like a bedroom that you might see in a house. The floor was covered in a kind of heavy-duty dark commercial carpeting that would be easy to clean and it would be exceptionally durable.

The room had a small sink with a small mirror directly over the sink. Each room had a paper towel dispenser, a paper cup holder and a tiny trash can at the right side of the sink. It had everything that a person really needed to survive for a few days. It amazed me that the walls inside of the cavern were all finished with sheetrock and painted plaster just like you would find inside of any big building. It was not something that you would expect to see inside of a cave.

Each bed had a crisp white bottom sheet, a pillow and two army-type blankets. As I started to drift off I thought, "These beds are really quite comfortable and it is so quiet here," and that was the last thing that I remembered.

SIXTEEN

The Conference

We were awakened out of a sound sleep by a knock on the door. I could see my watch by the light of the glowing night light. It was 7:18. We had been asleep all afternoon.

I climbed down from my bunk and without opening the door I ask, "Who is it?" The door had no locks, but I still didn't want anyone to just barge in on us.

"My name is Nathaniel Taylor and I have a message for you from Dr. Benjamin Keyes." As I opened the door Mr. Taylor handed me a white folded letter from Dr. Keyes. It said, "Could you please return to the lab within a half an hour. I have some very important information that I feel you would find interesting."

"You can tell Dr. Keyes that we will be there," I told Mr. Taylor. After the young man left we stopped by the restrooms to freshen up before seeing the doctor. I found a brush, a tooth brush, and some toothpaste in a neat little package under the sink. Within a few minutes I met my husband outside the restrooms and we were ready to go see Dr. Keyes.

"I wonder what Dr. Keyes wants to see us for," I said to my husband.

"I don't know, but I'm sure we'll soon find out," My husband said mockingly. "I can hardly wait, because judging from everything else that has happened today I am sure it will be something very baffling and weird."

When we arrived at the lab facility Nathaniel Taylor was standing at the entrance door waiting to escort us in to see Dr. Keyes. He took us down a narrow hallway and into a massive conference room near the back of the laboratory. It was not just Dr. Keyes that was there in the huge hall. The room was filled with many prominent people from around the state that I could recognize from the television or the newspaper. I instantly recognized many of the hometown mayors and the Governor of Idaho.

There were several rows of people that were dressed in the blue lab jumpsuits that we had seen earlier working down in the laboratory. I also noticed many rows of people in sheriff's uniforms, the state police, many firemen, military uniforms and various rows of men in dark suits that were probably from government agencies.

I could tell that people had come in from all over the world. The newspaper had reported that they were conferring with meteorologists from several different countries and they too were at the conference.

The reporters and cameramen from many different stations were standing all around the outside rows. Apparently the answer to the windstorm problems was about to be exposed, because the cameramen stood ready with cameras focused to tell the nation the answer to the strange phenomenon that had been taking over this small rural community.

The room was a huge pavilion type auditorium and it was completely filled with people from all walks of life. I could tell that many of them were farmers, local merchants, and families. I had no idea what was going on, but I knew that it was something big. As I looked around the room the expression on everyone's face was solemn and blank. The people looked tired and scared and I'm sure that every one else in the room had a lot more knowledge of what was going on then we did. We weren't even from around here. We just came to find our friends and ended up in this cavern.

Dr. Keyes was sitting directly in front of us at a head table. He looked pale and exhausted. He smiled a weak smile and nodded his head towards us as we walked in to find our seats. He had several people sitting on both sides of him and I assumed they were either there as speakers or to be some sort of moral support. The room was packed with people so I knew something very important was about to happen. They asked everyone to be seated and then one by one he introduced the people sitting at the front table.

After all of the introductions were made Dr. Keyes introduced his first speaker, it was a scientist by the name of Dr. Roberta Tomlin, the person sitting directly on his right.

Dr. Keyes sat down and Dr. Tomlin went to the podium. "Thank you all for coming today," Dr. Tomlin began. "I am part of the team that came to Idaho from Penn State University to try to find out what

118

has been causing the severe weather problems that have been occurring in this area."

She said, "I am an atmospheric scientist or a meteorologist specializing in climatology. A climatologist attempts to discover and explain the impacts of climate. Our team of specialists has been working on the situation here in Tower County for the past several days and Dr. Keyes felt that it was time for us to include every one of you in on the results that we have accumulated so far," she told the audience.

"Our team had been looking into several different reasons that might have been the cause for the disastrous occurrences here in this community. But everything that we suspected as the problem did not fit together. Nothing we had been working on made any sense until today. That is why we were hesitant to present anything to you until now." She shook her head before going on, "This morning it was brought to our attention that there was a fast moving black cloud mass that had been seen out near the wind turbines."

She went on, "We had all studied and dissected the huge computer screens many times, but not one of us had noticed the shadowy fast moving clouds until today when they were pointed out to us. With so much wind turbulence that minute dark mass just seemed insignificant up against everything else that we had been looking for."

"But after the dark cloud masses were brought to out attention we went back over the screens from the past week and we noticed the dark mass appeared in several different segments, but no one had ever noticed them before." She continued, "We had all been focusing our attention on the assumption that the wind had been causing the turbines to rotate much faster than normal, because that is the way the turbines were created to work. But the winds were not blowing from the right direction and that is what has been so confusing to our team. We are

119

used to solving difficult weather problems, but we had never before experienced anything like what has been going on here in Idaho."

"We realize now after looking at things from a different perspective that there was no wind to make the turbines go. That is why we were having such a difficult time figuring out the source of the problem."

She said, "When we started looking over all of the past screens we found that the dark cloud masses appeared many times during the daylight hours, but always on the back side of the wind turbines. So we still could not figure out the connection between the dark cloud masses and the wind problems until we were forced to dissect the situation and approach it from a different direction."

She continued, "For the past several hours we have had some of the top meteorologists and scientists from all over the world working with us here in the safety location as well as by satellite to help us find the connection between the dark clouds and the wind problems."

The doctor sincerely stated, "It might first appear that a small dark cloud mass would be insignificant in the overall complexity of the turbulent winds, because that is how it appeared to us. But that one small piece of evidence was the key to help us connect the dots to figure out what was going on here in Tower County."

"So that is why we are here," I said to myself. "I am the person who told them about the dark cloud mass."

Dr Tomlin continued on, "We were looking for a weather problem, because that is what we were sent here to do. But we now realize that the turbulent winds were not caused by any severe weather patterns. We discovered that something else is causing the mystery winds. The wind was not making the wind turbines go as they were designed to do; the wind turbines were creating the wind."

You could hear people gasping and murmuring all around the huge auditorium. I leaned over to my husband and whispered, "What does she mean that the wind turbines are what is creating the severe winds?"

"I don't know. Something would have to be malfunctioning inside of each tower to make every one of the turbines go out of control at the same time and that doesn't make any sense. In fact I'm sure that would be impossible," my husband whispered back to me.

Dr. Tomlin then said, "Dr Keyes has several points that he now needs to share with you." She sat down and Dr. Keyes moved back to the microphone.

He solemnly stated, "Dr. Tomlin has shared with you about the dark cloud masses that were discovered in several of the computer screen segments. Well, earlier today we magnified the sound that was coming from the dark mass and we heard a loud buzzing sound that sounded like bees. When I first heard the deafening sound coming from the dark cloud mass it didn't make a lot of sense to me. So we magnified the tone several times and it sounded like we were all trapped inside of a giant beehive. The reverberation was so distinct that it was overwhelming."

He continued, "When we first became aware of the tiny dark mass that had been seen out by the wind turbines; we enlarged the mass on the screen and we could tell that the mass was composed of millions of tiny individual pieces and it was not one solid mass like it first appeared. But after hearing the loud buzzing sound from inside the mass we immediately dismissed the fact that the sounds could really be the sounds of a beehive. In a normal beehive the bees would be too small for us to actually see each individual bee from the distance that our cameras were placed."

He continued, "When we enlarged the computer screens numerous times to get a better picture of the proposed bees we were shocked to see the actual size of each individual bee. Each bee was several times larger than what a normal bee should actually measure."

Dr. Keyes sighed and he paused for a minute before going on, "After consulting with an entomologist from Washington we realized that the bees would actually have to be crossbred numerous times to be the size that had appeared on our cameras from such a distance."

Dr. Keyes looked down at his notes for a few seconds before going on, "The entomologist has been working on a program with honeybees to try to enlarge the bees so that they can produce a larger quantity of honey. The doctor at the university told me that the honeybees have been diminishing because of what they are calling the 'colony collapse disorder.' That is why the scientists have been working on several programs to crossbreed the bees from different countries so that they can build up the honeybee population again."

Dr Keys said, "The doctor at the university told me that the reason they are working so hard to crossbreed the honeybee and to enlarge the colonies is because we all depend on the honeybees to pollinate flowers and plants. The scientists that are working on the honeybee projects fear that we would lose as much as 2/3 of our daily plant foods if we no longer have the honeybee colonies. Honey is a pure and natural food that is often written about all the way back to Bible times."

"The doctor in Washington told me that honeybees like untouched pastures much like the plains that the wind turbines are located on. Bees thrive in a field with wildflowers and clover," Dr. Keyes told the audience.

"That being said the entomologist also told me that when they have crossbred the honeybees they have become more aggressive and unmanageable," Dr. Keyes stated. "When I first heard the loud buzzing sound as we magnified it through the computer screens, we identified the dark cloud as honeybees. It reminded me of something that had happened a few days ago when the military brought in the first casualties."

Dr. Keyes then stated, "The volunteers found two bodies buried under piles of rubble after the wind had blown their barn over on top of them. Because the barn was blown down and they were buried beneath it, we assumed that is how they had died. But when I read over their death certificates signed by the coroner it stated that their bodies were covered in unidentified massive bites. When I first read the report I thought that their bodies had been ravaged by some type of insect after they were already dead; because they had been left on their property for several days before they could be retrieved.

I dismissed their deaths to be accidental and I assumed that they were killed by their collapsed barn and so we reported their deaths as being caused by the violent windstorms."

"Today after I was told about the giant bees I went back to the coroner's report and read everything again." Dr. Keyes told everyone, "I discovered that the names of the two people that were killed were Franklin and Josephine Faber. After doing a background check on the couple we discovered that their rural farm was the last property on the end of the lane and it was located right up next to the Tower County wind farm. The Fabers were very private people and they rarely had any company, very few people knew anything about them because they always kept to themselves."

He went on, "They had purchase an old run down farm house about three years ago and they never went into any of the small towns around the area. No one had heard of Franklin and Josephine Faber before they were killed. I was told that when they needed anything they drove all the way to Pocatello or Twin Falls to purchase groceries, clothing, and gas."

"Our investigators also learned that they had never talked to anyone in Pocatello or Twin Falls either," he continued. "They were truly private people and that is probably the reason why they had chosen the isolated property so far away from everyone. They didn't want anyone else around.

The small acreage that they had purchased had unworkable soil and it was covered in large lava rock with huge patches of field grass and scattered wildflowers. The only person that ever drove all the way to the end of their lane was the mail carrier and he only went out that way when he had mail for them which was about every two weeks and he rarely saw the couple. He knew that they had a few farm animals, but that was really all he knew about the Fabers."

"It was actually the sheriff who discovered the collapsed barn after the winds had first started. He was out checking on every single property to make sure that everyone was all right after the terrible windstorms had started. He came upon the Faber farm and discovered that there was no one around, but their barn was totally destroyed. The sheriff cautiously walked around the premises and then returned to town because the winds were already quite severe."

"When he got back to town he learned that there were two people who were suppose to be living on the Faber property. Since he had not found them when he was out there he decided that they had either left town because of the winds or they had been buried under the old barn.

Three days after the sheriff had visited the Faber farm a group of volunteers discovered the two mutilated bodies of Franklin and Josephine Faber. Both bodies had been destroyed by substantial insect bites. As I said we thought that they were from bugs living on the property and they had attacked the bodies after they were buried under the rubble of the barn," Dr. Keyes reported.

"After the background check we also discovered that Mr. Faber was an apiarist or beekeeper and several years ago he worked as a researcher with the doctor from Washington. The project that the researchers were working on was crossbreeding colonies of bees trying to create a new generation of honeybees. In their lab they put together Africanized honeybees with European honeybees. They were cross-breeding the bees trying to make larger more aggressive honeybees. They created larger queens and drones, but their behavioral traits made the bees less desirable for breeders because they became too hard to manage."

Dr. Keyes continued, "After reading all of the frightening information about the Fabers I took a team of scientist to the property this afternoon in an armored truck to retrieve any notes or information about the bees that the beekeeper had been working on. We know that most beekeepers with large quantities of bee hives keep notes on their bee colonies. Luckily Mr. Faber had an office type area out in his barn and the notebook was buried securely under the rubbish of the old barn, so it was still readable and intact."

Dr. Keyes told us, "We discovered thousands of hives on the farm. There were hives everywhere on the property, but they were all empty. We also found in his notebook where Mr. Faber had kept pages and pages of notes about his new generation of giant bees."

Dr. Keyes then let out a huge sigh before opening the large black notebook that he had retrieved from the Faber property earlier today. He said, "We found this book in the rubble this afternoon, it has all of the information and notes telling about Mr. Faber's research for the past several years."

The doctor continued, "We also found two dead horses along with Mrs. Faber's pet goat haphazardly buried in the rocky back yard. All three animals had multiple insect bites and they had been stung to death.

We retrieved the animal's bodies for observation and brought them back to this facility. The coroner did animal autopsies on all of the animals to show the cause of death, and they had died of massive poison from the bee stings. Hundreds of barbed stingers were still attached in each animal's hide."

Dr. Keyes began reading the beekeeper's documentation starting three years earlier. Dr. Keyes began, "It was obvious by Mr. Faber's notes that he was continuing on with the crossbreeding research that he had previously started in Washington several years ago. The research notes start out as Mr. Faber first purchased three beehives to begin his research."

As the doctor began to read from the notebook several people came in with trays filled with fresh coffee, hot tea, finger sandwiches and warm cookies. Dr Keyes stopped there and announced, "We will take a fifteen minute break before going on."

People throughout the room began to mumble about all the honeybee information that we had just been given. Everyone around us seemed shocked and afraid. I don't think anyone knew exactly what was going on because everything that had been said was so unreal. We weren't sure why the doctor was telling us about the large honeybees. What did the bees and the dark cloud masses have to do with all of the destruction caused by the violent windstorms. Nothing made a lot of sense.

SEVENTEEN

The Honeybee

We poured ourselves a cup of coffee and took a sandwich and a cookie and then sat back down. Apparently it was going to be a long night.

When we got started again Dr. Keyes quickly went back to reading the journal and he read several notes out of the notebook that had been written years earlier. He then flipped forward to a more recent time and started reading the notes from a few days ago.

The Life Cycle of the giant Honeybee

Franklin Faber (Apiarist)

May 1ˢᵗ the crossbreeding of the colonies has been very successful. My new generation of bees is four times larger than my original honeybees that I purchased three years ago. The colonies have multiplied by the millions and I now have over 6,000 honey producing hives and I am building several new hives each day. I am so excited because I will go down in history as the famous entomologist that saved the honeybee population. My life's work has been a success.

May 2nd the queens in each cell are laying double the amount of eggs and thus every colony is producing thousands of individual bees. They are reproducing so fast that I am having a difficult time keeping every nest site clean, dry and protected from the weather the way that I should. I work from early morning until late each night just trying to keep my hives healthy and alive, but it is getting more difficult each day.

May 3rd the giant bees are fascinating to watch. They are so much larger than a regular honeybee that I can easily track all of their movements in effortless detail. They are absolutely beautiful. I wish I had another entomologist to share my results with. I am still not clear why the bees are reproducing at such a rapid pace; I have no concrete reasoning to document their hasty reproduction.

May 4th the larger honeybees appear to be getting more aggressive daily. It is a little alarming. They each appear to have a mind of their own and I have never experienced behavior such as this in my previous bees.

May 5th the weather is getting warmer and I can see a difference in the aggression of the bees each day. They seem stressed and unsettled. It is odd, but the bees appear to be reacting to the light humming of the wind turbines just south of the farm. I don't remember ever having that problem with my hives before.

May 6th this has been a bad day for the hives, I can just tell that something is wrong. They seem to be very agitated and almost angry with the other bees in the hives. They dive at each other in a kind of fighting type action. This behavior is not normal in bees, because they usually work together in harmony.

May 7th with the larger bees I have noticed that the vibration is multiplied many times when all of the bees began to buzz in unison. The wings of the honeybee beat 200 times a second to create the buzzing sound. Multiplied by several million times it makes the sound almost unbearable because once they start this mass communicating it shakes everything that is close by.

I've had several things vibrate and crash off of the shelves in my barn. The buzzing gets so violent that the coffee will splash right out of my coffee cup no matter where I have it sitting. The considerable buzzing frightens the horses so bad that they will take off running and stand out in the far corner of the field panting and wheezing.

When the bees begin the massive humming all of the ground around them begins to tremble and it feels much like being in the center of a huge earthquake. The colonies are reproducing at such a rapid pace that the humming continually gets stronger and stronger. This afternoon I was actually thrown to the ground by the incalculable trembling. Within just a few days I have began to fear that I am recklessly losing all control of my hives.

May 8th the humming of the bees is almost like a rebellious type of sound. They react off of each other the way that a massive group of people act when a riot is about to ensue. They just get louder and louder and they sound angrier and angrier as each hive joins in the rebellious thunder.

May 9th the weather has gotten warmer overnight and it is now almost summer like weather and the bees are getting restless. I can see a high stress level in all of the hives. They are extremely nervous and appear very agitated. At times they frighten me, because they do not respond the same way as other honeybees respond. Stressed bees will try to abscond. When they get stressed the entire colony leaves the hive and they will relocate, each queen will leave and the entire colony will follow her.

May 10th the bees actually appear to be communicating with the wind turbines. I am beginning to question what I have created. Not only are the bees four times the size of a regular honeybee, they are multiplying at a very unhealthy pace and there is no way for me to stop them. I don't know how to stop the rapid reproduction, because I do not know what started it in the first place.

May 11th if the weather was colder I would just let the new, younger bees freeze, but the weather has gotten so warm that the bees act like they no longer need me.

May 12th I found my wife's pet goat dead out by the barn this morning. The enormous bees had attacked the goat and had taken it down. My wife was so distraught; she wants me to dispose of all of the beehives. She says she has a bad feeling about the giant bees. Our property has a lot of huge lava boulders so I buried the goat in the backyard the best that I could.

May 13th the angry honeybees flew at me this morning and I was terrified. I think my wife is right; I have created a colony of killers. I know this is a weird thing to say, but the giant bees act like they are watching my every move.

May 14th I have made up my mind to dispose of all of the beehives tonight, because this morning the bees killed our two horses. The horses were mutilated with numerous bites. I buried the horses in the back field. I tried to dig a hole with my backhoe, but it was very difficult. I then covered the dead horses up with dirt. The horses were large and healthy, yet the bees took them down. I had a difficult time burying our horses because they are so bulky and our ground is so hard, but I covered them up with as much dirt as I could collect.

I now fear for our lives, because if the bees would kill the horses, they would also kill us. I wish I could go to someone for help, but I have avoided everyone in the community and besides I have created these monsters myself. It is up to me to take care of this problem. My wife was right about the bees, they are killers. So, I promised her that I will destroy every one of the hives this evening when it gets dark and the bees are dormant. I plan to smoke the beehives first to calm the bees down then I will torch every one of my hives while I still can and the bees are still in one location.

I have never used the smoker on the giant honeybees because these colonies react so differently than other colonies have in the past. I hope that the smoke works on them. I have never been afraid of any of the others bees that I have worked with. Every beekeeper knows that knowledge of bees is your best line of defense, but this new string of bees seems to be thinking on their own and they do not respond the way that other colonies have.

Torching all of the hives will be a big undertaking, but my wife said that she would help me. I dread to think what would happen if the monstrosities that I have created were to relocate and to continue to reproduce at the same rapid pace that they have been reproducing. There would be no way to stop them and they would destroy everything in their path.

"That is where the notes abruptly end," said Dr. Keyes. "We have conversed with several entomologist to find out what they think has happened to the giant bees." Dr. Keyes shook his head back and forth and shrugged his shoulders in disbelief, "They think that the bees were stressed and they relocated inside of the wind turbines, because the beekeeper's notes state that they were communicating with the humming of the windmills."

Dr. Keyes again shook his head back and forth and told us, "We are quite sure that it is the bees that also killed a number of range cattle that were grazing out near the wind farms, because the cattle were all killed shortly before all the wind storms began. Most likely when the bees left the beehives they first killed Franklin and Josephine Faber while they were still in the barn preparing to destroy the hives. Then the colonies attacked the cattle on their way out to the wind turbines. That would explain why the cattle were reported to have extensive insect bites all over them."

"After we did the research about the bees, everything makes more sense. Bees are relatively dormant at night and that is why the winds would disappear after sunset," Dr. Keyes reported. "I am so sorry to be the one to have to tell you about all of the horrendous things that we have discovered in the past few days. Our team came here to Idaho to give you professional advice on climatology, but after putting all of the pieces together things are completely different than we first supposed."

He went on, "The strange events that have been going on here are completely beyond our understanding. We have seen so much destruction and loss in the past few days it is absolutely incomprehensible, so at this time I would like to introduce you to an expert that will share some information with us on the construction of the wind turbines. Please help me welcome Harold Pinson a specialist with the wind turbine project."

Mr. Pinson then stood up and came to the microphone and said, "I was the lead project manager for the Windsor Wind Farm that is located about 430 feet above the Snake River Canyon. I worked for the Windsor Energy Project. The Windsor Wind Farm sits on 8,000 acres of private land in southeast Tower County and it has 48 renewable energy wind turbines."

He then turned to a large computer screen that was on the wall directly behind him. Mr. Pinson began, "I have spent several hours today studying the laboratory computer screens showing the wind turbines where the dark cloud masses were detected." He continued, "I have also listened to the magnified noise of what sounds like the inside of a giant beehive that was recorded coming from the dark cloud mass. Although I am not a specialist on beekeeping I did take some time this afternoon to do a little research on beehives and honeybees."

Then he showed us a giant outline of a wind turbine on the big screen behind him. "Let me first explain to you how a wind turbine works," he said. "Every turbine has a pole or tower that is the center of the wind turbine that holds the blades up in the air. On the top of each pole or tower is a nacelle which is the housing for all of the parts of the wind turbine. Outside of the nacelle are the anemometers or wind vanes which tell the turbine control system how fast the wind is and in which direction it is blowing. The blade assembly is called the rotor. The pitch motors in the hub allow the angle of the blades. The final component inside the nacelle is the generator which is connected to the gearbox and the brake. The gearbox is responsible for converting that speed to around 1,500 RPM rotation energy and converts it into electrical power. The power is then sent out of the turbine through the cables running down the length of the tower."

Mr. Pinson went on, "After studying the pictures of the wind turbines of the past few days I estimate that the blades were rotating at a rate of at least forty times the maximum speed that they were originally made to rotate, acting much like a giant fan. The bees make the giant turbines work the exact opposite of the way they were designed to work.

The wind turbines are supposed to be driven by the wind; they are not supposed to produce massive winds. Also, after documenting the weather on the back side of the wind turbines I observed that the winds were out of the southeast at only around 15 to 17 MPH. Thus, proving that the weather was not what was creating the aggressive rotation of the blades."

"The violent winds were not created by strong winds patterns from severe weather. The strong winds were caused by something making the giant wind turbines malfunction; something peculiar and uncharacteristic of the normal wind projects. It is so abnormal that the producers of the wind farms could have never foreseen this to happen with any of our wind turbines," He went on.

He added, "There are approximately 20,000 onshore turbines in just the United States alone, not counting all of the other successful wind projects that we have all over the world. And we have never had anything like this happen before. Several companies have had trouble with birds and frequent noise humming from the turbines, but as a whole the wind turbine projects have been rated a huge success."

Mr. Pinson sadly stated, "This afternoon I along with five of my colleagues have concluded that the wind turbines had been invaded by the giant honeybee colonies from Franklin Faber's beehives."

He went on, "As unbelievable as all of this seems we think that the bees entered the wind turbines through the nacelle and relocated in the gearbox converting the wind speed by the massive vibration noise that Mr. Faber had written about in his journal." Mr. Pinson concluded, "Our conclusion to this shocking situation is that millions of giant killer bees have taken over all 48 wind turbines of Tower County, thus creating the massive winds."

Mr. Pinson shook his head and sadly said, "After reading the notes of Mr. Faber on how rapidly the bees are reproducing we have concluded, that is why the winds would continue to get worse everyday. There are more bees that communicate, thus making more vibration, disabling the anemometers, making the blades rotate faster creating stronger winds."

He then paused and briefly closed his eyes for a few seconds before going on, "I am sorry to inform you that last night two of our specialists were attacked by the giant bees while they were trying to shut the power systems down on turbines one and two."

He shook his head back and forth before going on, "Only yesterday, my colleagues and I decided to have our turbine specialists go through and manually dismantle every single one of the wind turbines. We hoped that by shutting down all of the turbines, we could get to the root of the destructive winds."

"The specialists were just getting started when they encountered the bees. When the two specialists entered the turbines we didn't know anything about the bees. One of the specialists died at the scene and the second actually crawled away, climbed into his work truck and radioed back that they had run into problems. He continued to scream into the radio. "No, no, no...Help me; help me they are everywhere," he shouted before he passed out.

"Both men were married with small children and they had lived in Pocatello most of their lives." Mr. Pinson sadly told the audience. "It was dark by the time we retrieved the men from the two turbine sites. We believe that the first man was attacked and he fell to his death from high up on the ladder inside turbine two. He had to be identified by his work clothes and his name across the pocket of his shirt, because he had been stung so many times."

I leaned over to my husband as I remembered that poor man that was screaming in the hallway and I quietly whispered in Darrell's ear, "That must be the man that we saw in the hallway earlier today." I said trying to keep the tears from running down my face.

My husband shook his head up and down. "I'm sure it was, and that poor guy probably won't live either," My husband whispered back to me. "He looked so terrible."

I then realized that Mr. Pinson was still talking and he said, "Now that we have learned about the bees our specialists could go in during the night in protective clothing, gloves and a hooded suit or a hat and veil and shut down every one of the wind turbines. Our greatest fear now is that if we turn off the turbines and the humming stops that the millions of bees will then relocate. They could easily travel in any direction and we would lose our chances of ever being able to destroy the colonies."

"After reading over Mr. Faber's notes we have concluded that these particular bees cannot be controlled by smoke. During a private meeting a couple of hours ago we acknowledged that Mr. Faber attempted to smoke the bees to calm them down before torching them. We have to assume that the smoke didn't work. Because when he tried to smoke the bees to make them calmer, they got more vicious. That is when they turned on Mr. Faber and his wife and killed them."

He went on, "By the next day when the bees had entered the wind turbines and the violent winds began, the old barn blew down on top of their dead bodies. The barn was old and run down and it could have easily just collapsed and have been blown over by the strong winds. That is why their deaths were documented as being caused by the winds.

Their property is the closest farm to the turbines so it would be the first property to get the full force of the violent winds. Naturally, Dr.

Keyes and his team had reported that the Fabers had been killed by the severe windstorms, when actually they were dead before the winds even started."

"After viewing the screens from the past several days we discovered that the bees seem to stay fairly close around the turbines as long as the turbines are on and they can communicate with the humming sound. All of the dark cloud masses that we documented seeing rarely traveled more than a few miles or so before returning to the turbines. It appears as long as the turbines are working we have some control over the colonies," Mr. Pinson stated.

"The concern that our specialists have at this point is that the turbines may malfunction from rotating too fast. As the bees rapidly reproduce and make the blades rotate faster they overwork the complete system of the wind turbines. We have actually had a few of the giant turbines catch on fire from rotating faster than they were intended to do."

"The turbines that caught fire were located in a torrential stormy area, and the winds were much stronger than we had anticipated they would ever be. The blades were rotating faster than they were ever intended to do," he said.

"Our third concern is that the blades may just completely stop working from all of the extra movement and abuse on the systems." He went on, "When the wind turbines were originally designed they were made strong enough to withstand immense hurricane-type winds, but my team of specialists are worried about how long the blades can keep up this high speed rotation.

Most wind turbines that are in the center of a massive storm are only rotating over capacity for a short time and then the storm is over. This situation is different because the bees have manipulated the wind turbines everyday for several days in a row. Every aspect of the turbine's design has been severely over-working for many days, and we are fearful of what might happen."

"Of course we have not done any testing on such a bizarre situation, so we do not have any data to let us know what will happen. That concludes all of the information that I have," Mr. Pinson said gently nodding his head up and down as he turned around to go sit down.

Dr. Keyes once again stood before the assembly and said, "We will be having an open discussion after we take a thirty minute break. I want to give everyone enough time to digest some of the unbelievable things that we have discussed here tonight. Take a few minutes to think about what you have been told and I look forward to any response or questions that any of you may have when we return."

After Dr. Keyes concluded his presentation and sat down the entire room broke out into an enormous vocal rumble. Everyone was talking to each other at one time. The news stations had shut off their cameras quite some time ago. They must have concluded that with such frightening information it was not a good idea to spread panic throughout the listening audiences just yet.

With all of the confusing information that we had been given the general consensus was outright panic. I doubt that anyone in this conference room came here today with idea that the massive wind problems in Tower County were created by a crazy beekeeper and his newly crossbred giant killer bees. I know that when I first noticed the dark cloud masses in the sky I never thought of bees and I am sure that none of the scientist would have guessed that either.

We have all heard of the dreadful killer bees from Africa, but it is hard to believe that they are now here in Idaho.

EIGHTEEN

Disaster

During the break we walked down the hall to the restrooms and talked about some of the unusual things that we had been told at the conference. I told my husband, "I feel so sorry for Dr. Keyes. He seems like such a nice person and he has just kind of been thrown into the middle of this mess. I'm sure he never dreamed he would have to deal with something like this when he came to Idaho as a meteorologist."

We were just headed back to the conference auditorium when all of the lights began to flash on and off and loud sirens roared throughout the building. A vibrant voice then shouted over the loudspeaker, "BREACH... BREACH... BREACH... THE FACILTY HAS BEEN

COMPROMISED. I REPEAT THE FACILTY HAS BEEN COMPROMISED."

People in blue jumpsuits were hastily scrambling up and down the halls. They were shouting and screaming at each other and at first we couldn't understand what they were saying. Finally we realized they were shouting code six, code six, as they screamed at each other and ran past us racing to their destination.

Of course we had no idea what code six meant, but we could tell by the panic in their expressions that something very alarming was going on. We didn't know whether to go back to our room, stay right where we were or go on down to the conference room and sit down and wait. Finally, a man in a blue jumpsuit nudged my husband's arm and said, "Get to the safety area immediately."

My husband told the man, "I'm sorry, but we don't know where the safety area is."

The man then shouted back to us as he hurried away, "Head towards the cafeteria and the safety area is directly across the hall from the cafeteria."

We instantly did as the man advised and we turned around and headed back in the direction where we had just come from. As we scurried along the open hallway we came to the reception desk and the desk was now empty. The young man was already gone that had been sitting at the desk only a few moments ago when we came by.

We headed towards the cafeteria and as we went around the corner we saw armed military guards posted at several different locations. They were stiffly standing at attention prepared for any emergency that might arise.

One of the soldiers opened the heavy door for us and we hesitantly entered into a long dark cave-like hallway. We cautiously walked down the dark hall for probably 100 feet until we came to another large set of heavy doors that were also guarded by two soldiers.

Once again the soldiers opened the massive doors for us and we entered into an enormous open cavern. This part of the cave was very rustic and it was probably in its natural form. It did not have finished walls and carpeted floors like much of the rest of the cave that we had been in.

It actually looked like the inside of a dark cave. It was damp, very dark and it smelled like mud. It was probably the largest part of the entire facility. As we walked into the gigantic room and our eyes slowly started to adjust we recognized many of the people that had been at the conference with us.

There were also several sections of children sitting off to one side. An adult was positioned in-between every few children. "These must be the students and teachers that were rescued from the grade school several days ago," I thought to myself. "I recall the newspaper stating that many families had refused to send their kids to school. This could not be an entire school, so these must be the few students who went on to school after they were reported closed."

Everyone was quietly sitting around the room on metal folding chairs. I quickly estimated that there were probably 300 to 400 people waiting in the large cave area. They were all extremely silent as they sat and waited. Not one person talked to us or even acknowledged that we were there as we walked across the room to find a chair.

Everyone just sat quietly and looked very frightened and lost. Darrell and I sat down on the first empty chairs available. Even as we sat there in this room full of strangers the lights flickered on and off and the sirens continued to roar.

Out of all of the rooms that we had been in since our arrival at the safety location you could tell that this room was definitely the inside of a mountain. The walls were unfinished and the floor was solid dirt. But as I looked around I decided that this was probably the safest place in the whole cave. It was musty and damp and you could instantly tell that this was the place to come if the facility had an emergency and people wanted to feel safe.

"I wonder what is going on," I whispered to my husband. "They said that the problem was bees, do you think the bees have invaded the safety location? Would that set off all of the alarms?"

"Who knows," my husband said as he shrugged his shoulders. "But I'm sure we are safe in here; at least from the bees. I would think this dark, damp cave would be the last place that bees would want to go."

No one else really talked to each other; every person in there just sat quietly and waited. After being in the cave for awhile I was starting to get a little tense. Finally the sirens stopped and the lights stopped flickering, but still we had not been given the okay to leave the room.

Two armed guards stood posted at the doors, both on the inside and I assumed the other two guards were still on the other side. And as I looked around I realized that the doors they were guarding were the only way out. Apparently, this room was the end of the cavern and it didn't go any deeper into the mountain. There was no way out except through the heavy double doors and down the dark hallway to get to civilization. "My dad was a captain of the Boise Fire Department. I wonder what the fire inspector would have to say about the exits in this room," I smiled to myself.

I was starting to feel a little claustrophobic. I hated the feeling of being trapped inside of a dark room and not being able to leave at will. Being trapped inside the dark cave was a very strange experience. We all just sat silently remaining imprisoned in the damp dungeon. I'm sure that everyone else was just like me, they were wondering what was happening on the other side of the door. The longer we waited the more frightening it became.

We knew that there were guards located both inside and outside of the doors, but it was so spooky sitting inside the cave impatiently waiting; we couldn't help but feel vulnerable. We had no idea what we were waiting for. The heavy door was closed and we couldn't see anything. If a terrorist or someone with guns came barging into the room, there would be absolutely nothing any of us could do to protect ourselves.

As my mind was thoroughly inundated with every kind of terrifying thought imaginable, the huge doors opened up and we were told that we could all exit to the outside hallway and wait. The hall in front of the cafeteria was large, open and well-lit so we welcomed the change.

Every person got up and politely shuffled to the hall to wait for additional instructions. I doubt that anyone minded waiting in the hallway, because it was so much better than sitting imprisoned in the dark cave room.

Darrell and I moved back up against the wall once we got out to the hallway by the cafeteria. We were trying to make room for other people and we wanted to stay out of everyone's way that might need to get by. As we stood there Dr. Tomlin came out of the safety room and stopped and stood right up next to us. I quietly asked her, "Excuse me, but do you know what a code six means?"

"Yes, a code six means the same thing in every one of the safety location facilities," she told me. "It means there is an invader on the premises and so they automatically put the entire facility in lock down. These facilities are used for all types of disasters. If there were a terrorist attack for instance, they like to corral everyone in the same location so that the military can protect them and they know right where everyone is."

She continued to tell us, "The safety room is the safest place in the whole facility because it is the original cave and it is usually the deepest part of the mountain. The military gets everyone to safety and then they take care of whatever needs to be taken care of and that way they know that the civilians are all protected."

As we stood there talking, the military police brought out a man in handcuffs and the man was screaming and wailing to the top of his lungs. He was just a normal looking guy; he didn't appear scary at all. He had no weapons and he didn't look like he could hurt anyone. The man was clean cut, handsome and dressed in a flannel shirt, Nike's and new Levi's; but he did look very disturbed about something.

My husband and I just stood there with our mouths open. This guy sure didn't look very threatening to us especially the way he was sobbing. As we stood there next to Dr. Tomlin, a man in a blue jumpsuit walked up to let her know what was going on.

Her co-worker told her, "That man's name is Jim Haynes; he is the brother of the wind turbine specialist that was killed by the bees yesterday. When he heard about his brother's death he went to the morgue to identify him. When he saw the horrible way that his brother had been killed, he just went berserk because his dead brother looked so terrible."

The man in the blue jumpsuit sadly went on, "Mr. Haynes is a military man and he has worked at this facility several different times, so he knew right where to go to reach the restricted area. He was so upset after seeing his brother that he didn't know what to do, so he lashed out the only way that he knew how. He even knew the security code to get into the restricted area so that is where he went."

The man in the blue jumpsuit went on, "After he saw his brother's mutilated body he went directly to the restricted area and began smashing up the place. He broke a leg off of a table and just started destroying everything because he was so distraught."

The man shook his head back and forth and wiped his eyes before saying, "When he started smashing all of the equipment, it set off of the emergency alarms and they shut everything down. No one was hurt, but he did an endless amount of damage to the computers and the electrical system. The emergency system had to take over after the electrical system went down."

"Oh that poor guy," Dr. Tomlin said covering her face with her hands. "This hideous situation just seems to go from one disaster to another." She looked at me with tears in her eyes and said, "I can't imagine seeing one of my family members after they had been attacked by these horrible creatures. I saw the two horses and the goat after they brought them in and I couldn't believe what I was seeing."

I sadly looked at Dr. Tomlin and shook my head up and down that I agreed. I knew exactly how atrocious they looked after the bees got through with them, because I had seen the man in the hall that had survived. I then closed my eyes and silently prayed for the brother that had been taken out in handcuffs and also for the man in the hallway that was mutilated so badly. I felt so sorry for both of them. Dr. Tomlin was right; this whole experience was a hideous situation.

I was startled as the loud speaker blared and gave the all-clear signal. We were excused to return to the auditorium. I felt half sick as we headed back towards the lecture hall. This powerless situation was just too much to endure. Darrell and I walked up towards the front of the room and took our places and sat down to wait.

We were some of the first people to return. Slowly the room began to fill back up, but I'm sure the code six alarms made many of the people question where they should be. I know it did us. In fact, after looking around the room I am not sure if every person returned after the break. A good portion of the room looked empty and there were several unoccupied chairs.

Apparently, while we were waiting in the hallway for the all-clear signal to sound, the side tables in the auditorium had been provided with English muffins, cinnamon rolls, donuts, little sausages and bacon and several types of fruit. They had coffee, hot tea, milk and several kinds of juices. For the first time in hours I looked down at my watch and realized it was morning. It was 5:17 A.M. There had been so much going on that we had again lost all track of time.

As Dr. Keyes took his place back on the stage he apologized for the disruption of the code six. With great composure he told everyone about the dead man's brother and tried to make excuses for the man for acting so distraught. He said, "Please let me apologize for the man who was arrested. He has experienced a terrible tragedy, not only did he come here tonight to identify his dead brother; but he was devastated by the revolting way that his brother had been killed. He couldn't help himself, he was so upset and he was lashing out in the only way that he could. This whole situation has gotten everyone so upset and the disaster isn't even over yet."

The doctor went on, "During the break I used the emergency military phone line and I contacted several beekeepers and the president of the county beekeepers organization to discuss our situation with them. They are on their way here and they should arrive sometime this afternoon."

"Also, the lead entomologist from Washington that I had spoken with yesterday, the man that had once worked on the crossbreeding of honeybees with Mr. Faber, will be arriving at the compound by 2:00 P.M. this afternoon. Now that we know what has caused the terrible windstorms, we have called in the professional bee experts to advise us on what we need to do now."

Dr. Keyes then told us, "Every one of the beekeepers told me the same thing about the colonies inside of the turbines. They said our main concern at the present time is to keep the bees in the wind turbines and not allow them to relocate or they could go anywhere."

He said, "The beekeepers said that if the bees relocate we will have a very difficult time ever finding them again, let alone trying to destroy them." He timidly told us, "They said if the bees abscond again the only way that we will be able to find them is by following the havoc that they create."

He solemnly told us, "They also told me that the only way that we will be able to completely get rid of the honeybees is to take care of every wind turbine of bees at the same time, because we will not get a second chance. They must all be destroyed at one time. They said if we started with only a couple of turbines at a time the other bees would relocate and we would lose our chance to destroy every one of them."

He commented, "It will be a huge undertaking to destroy all of the colonies at one time, but they said that is the only way that would be productive. The men will advise us what needs to be done when they arrive later on this afternoon."

Just as Dr. Keyes was ready to dismiss us for a few hours, one of the people from the lab came in and handed him an important message. Dr. Keyes let out a huge sigh and he put his left hand up to his face and kind of slid it down his cheek as he read the message.

Then he read the frightening note out loud to us and it said, "Dear Dr. Keyes, the honeybees in turbine seven are leaving. We have been carefully watching every turbine as you instructed us to do. And as we watched the turbines we could plainly see the colony masses in turbine seven are on the move. As far as we can tell they are the only colony that is moving so far. What should we do?"

Dr. Keyes looked at the audience and shrugged his shoulders and he said, "I'm sorry, this is exactly what we were trying to avoid. I will confer with the military and see what advice they have for us, because I have no idea how to stop bees from relocating."

He looked down at the messenger in the blue jumpsuit and said, "All I can say is keep a camera on them and track them as far as you can. And when the professional beekeepers get here they can advise us on what we need to do next."

Dr. Keyes then dismissed everyone until later on this afternoon after the beekeepers arrive.

Darrell and I decided to go back to our room and rest for a few hours. We hadn't eaten much, but at least we both had a cinnamon roll, fresh fruit and some bacon along with our coffee and juice, so that should be enough for now.

It crossed our minds to try to find our car and escape, but it was daytime and the severe winds were back again and we still weren't sure exactly how to find our way out. We didn't even know where we were, because we had driven into the complex between the two giant military vehicles and our vision was totally obscured.

Even if we could find our way out to the highway, I doubt we could find our way back to the safe-haven location. Besides, the thought of being out on the roads with the killer bees was even more terrifying than

149

getting lost. Plus we still hadn't found Suzanne and Gene and that is what we had come for. So, we walked back to our room and went to sleep.

NINEEEN

The Chopper

After everyone left the auditorium for the break the military radioed the Mountain Home Air Force Base for backup. Within minutes they had a chopper dispatched to track the swarm of killer bees to see where they would land. The chopper was in the air within a few minutes and they were warned to keep their distance and to retreat at once if the bees try to attack. They were told that their job was just to follow the colony and figure out where they land.

By now the news media had announced that the violent winds had been the result of a crossbred strand of Africanized killer bees, but the general public did not know how serious the problem really was. People were still not allowed back into the destroyed area and they had moved the safe-haven location all the way back to the main interstate.

151

For security reasons they were not letting anyone travel into the area until the violent winds were controlled and a solution to the killer bee crisis was over. It was just easier to keep everyone away from the restricted region until things could get settled. The entire region was still evacuated and absolutely no one was allowed into the vicinity. Even the police were restricted to the outskirts of town.

Although the authorities knew that people were anxious to get back to their properties, they were not ready to let them back into their homes. The destruction was so severe that it would take the community months to get things cleaned up and somewhat back to normal.

Even though the scientists had discovered the cause of the incomprehensible winds the problem had not yet been taken care of. The bees were still causing havoc with the wind gusts through the remaining turbines, so although they knew what had caused the violent winds the problems had not yet been solved.

Dr. Keyes was not trying to keep the bees a secret from anyone, he was genuinely afraid and he was being very cautious to avoid an all-out panic. If people had seen what some of us had seen in the past few days, the crowds would be uncontrollable, because the entire situation has been an unbelievable nightmare. The terrifying winds, the mutilated bodies, the dead animals, the destroyed homes, and all of the contaminated roads and ground are just more than a person can comprehend.

When they finally allow people to go back to their properties they will be in total shock from what they discover. The general public will never believe that all of the carnage has been caused by a giant mass of crossbred honeybees. I know because we have seen it and we cannot believe it.

The terrifying Africanized honeybees are much more menacing than anyone could even begin to imagine. They are not just mutated over-sized honeybees; they are demented and they would devour and kill anyone or anything that gets in their way. No living thing is safe as long as the millions of bees are still alive.

* * * *

The chopper from Mountain Home Air Force Base arrived at the designated location within minutes of their departure. They instantly spotted the swarm of bees soaring through the air across their radar screen. The pilots kept their distance as they were instructed, but they were overwhelmed when they saw how huge the swarm of bees appeared. The swarm covered the total screen. The pilots knew right away that there was something abnormal about the bees, because the swarm seemed several times larger than normal.

Within a few seconds after the chopper located the hive, the entire colony descended onto a giant tree stump that was up next to an old barn. The barn was located out in the center of a vast meadow full of wild flowers and clover. It was the perfect place for a colony of giant honeybees to set up their new beehive. They swarmed and landed on the sunlit side of the barn and spread out across the entire east wall of the old building. The abandoned barn was located in Rockland only a few miles south of the huge wind turbines.

* * * *

A short time later the military vehicles brought in the beekeepers and the entomologist from Washington. They got the exact location as to where they could find the giant colony and then they stepped into action to go and gather the huge honeybees.

Within minutes the beekeepers got dressed into their safety attire and were ready to head out to find the deadly hive. They had brought everything with them that they would need to collect the bees. Once they were on their way, the ground team radioed the chopper that they were approximately six minutes away and they would be there soon.

As the chopper canvassed the area to keep an eye on the bees, they noticed five dead antelope on top of a mound directly above where the bees had just landed. A few miles east they saw several dead cows also scattered throughout the field.

"What in the world is going on here?" the first pilot shouted to the other pilot. "Did you see all those dead animals? You don't think those bees did that do you?"

"I don't think so, bees don't usually kill other animals, but they did call them Africanized killer bees and the bees seem a lot bigger than a normal honeybee." The pilot got a strange look on his face, "And they did give us strict orders to keep our distance and to get out of here if the bees come after us," the second pilot replied. "Something is wrong here. This makes me really nervous, because if it was the bees that killed those animals, they had to kill them all in the short time that it took us to get into the air and get over here."

The first pilot then stated, "That means they can attack an animal and take it down within a few minutes." The two pilots looked at each other in total shock, "They are just like a swarm of locust consuming a field. I have never seen anything like that in my life. They really are killer bees."

"This is very disturbing. No wonder they wanted us to track them and not let them get away. I wonder how many other animals they have killed," the second pilot shouted. "Do you think we could outrun them if they decide to come after us?"

The first pilot shrugged his shoulders and then rapidly shook his head up and down and said, "Yeah, I'm sure we could outrun them as long as we got enough warning. But I hope we don't have to find out."

"Hey, I think I can see dust from the military vehicles coming this way," the second pilot hollered. "I sure hope it is them, because I am ready to get out of here. You better radio that we have spotted several dead animals directly in the wake of the swarm of bees. We'll let the authorities decide how the animals died," he added. "Be sure and give them the exact location otherwise no one on the ground will able to find them for awhile."

The ground team radioed that they had arrived at the hive's location and the chopper could now return to base. The pilots were more than ready to get out of there. After seeing all of the dead animals they were happy to be released to head back home.

"I hope they can really capture those killer bees," the first pilot responded as he hovered above the scene and watched the beekeepers unloading all of their gear. "After seeing what the bees are capable of, I sure wouldn't want to be one of the beekeepers trying to corral that irritated mass. I hope they know what they are doing," he said shaking his head back and forth rapidly.

The second pilot questioned, "Can you imagine if those killers landed in a busy city? A city filled with children playing outside and dogs and cats running all around? After actually seeing the damage that they are capable of I think those bees would go after anyone. This whole situation just makes my skin crawl. Let's get out of here." Then they gladly left the terrorizing bees to the beekeepers and flew back to the Mountain Home Air Force Base trying to erase the horrible images out of their minds.

TWENTY

The Beekeepers

The beekeepers planned to try to take the hive alive if possible so that they could study the giant bees and find out just exactly how to dispose of them. Actually, killing the bees would be very difficult for every one of the beekeepers, because they had all spent many years working with hives and trying to save the honeybee. Deciding to destroy them was not natural for them. Normally, they would do anything to keep the bees alive if possible.

The bees had chosen the warm protected sunny wall to sprawl out on. The barn was old and it probably hadn't been used in years, but it was an ideal place for a massive swarm of Africanized honeybees to abscond and relocate. The worker bees had quickly surrounded the queen as she found the giant tree stump and then the rest of the hive tried to fall into

157

place, but they were so crowded that they were forced to spread out and cover the entire side of the large barn.

The first time the beekeepers saw the massive swarm that engulfed the barn they were awestruck by the size of the hive. They were completely overwhelmed by the sheer size of the giant creatures. It was like staring at a scene from a prehistoric time. The bees were unbelievable. They were so enormous that you could see their every movement as they crept around on the barn wall. The beekeepers just stared at the magnified bulk of the huge bees.

Of course none of the beekeepers or the military people had ever seen bees of this scale. Not only were the bees several times larger than any normal honeybee, but a typical colony usually contains 8,000 to 60,000 bees and the beekeepers estimated this one hive alone to range around 500,000 bees or more. It was difficult to guess.

The beekeepers just gawked in disbelief. They were so impressed by the uniqueness of the giant bees that they could not believe what they were seeing. When they finally snapped to their senses and remembered what they had been sent there to do they took turns duct taping the other person's sleeves, pant legs and any other exposed areas. They didn't dare take a chance on letting the bees find any open or exposed area because they knew that the bees were not to be trusted. They had been told that they had already killed several animals and at least three people.

From the beginning, the doctor from Washington gave commands and ordered the beekeepers around. He told them what equipment to unload and exactly where they needed to put everything. He seemed very knowledgeable so everyone did exactly as they were told.

Dr. Scans was a well-known entomologist from Washington, so they were all glad to be able to use his expertise. The beekeepers had read many articles about Dr. Scans and they knew that he was a gifted scientist. They were honored to be able to work with him on this honeybee project. Every one of the beekeepers had heard of him and respected his work.

They knew that he had a reputation of being brilliant, but he was also known to be abrupt and rude. He had been working on the crossbreeding of bees for many years so they were glad to follow whatever he said. He knew more about the Africanized killer bees than anyone else did so they gladly listened to his commands, no matter how offensive he appeared. It was obvious that he didn't work well with other people.

Beekeepers are usually very jovial workers because they love working with their hives. They like to share their knowledge with other people and especially young children. The art of beekeeping is very fascinating to young people and most beekeepers welcome sharing their success. They like teaching other people how to work with the bee hives so that beekeeping does not become extinct. Beekeepers encourage people to learn how to take care of the hives and they enjoy passing their knowledge on to someone else.

The men knew that they had a very serious mission that needed to be taken care of and Dr. Scans was the only one who knew exactly what to do. They could tell that this hive was so massive that it would be completely overwhelming if one person tried to conquer the task alone. They knew that that it would take every one of them working together to get the hive into the boxes. Then they would have to take on the enormous challenge of the bees in the giant wind turbines.

The beekeepers knew that it would be easier to capture the swarm at this time because they had just recently settled. It would take every one of them working together to get the job accomplished, so no mater how abrupt the doctor became all of the beekeepers followed his demands.

Dr. Joseph Scans told everyone except for the beekeepers to remain inside one of the enclosed military vehicles for safety. He did not want to have to worry about anyone getting hurt or in his way. He was so bossy that he even ordered the military personal around, but everyone did as they were told. The men were probably more than happy to stay protected inside the vehicle and not be out near the deadly bees.

Of course the beekeepers were the only ones that were covered in the protective clothing, so they were the only ones that were truly safe outside of the vehicle anyway.

This was a stronger strand of bees and the giant bees had taken down many large animals. So, the beekeepers were not even sure if the normal protective clothing that they were wearing would even be enough if they were under attack, but it was all that they had.

Every one of them knew that this particular process was going to take all of their knowledge and their expertise. But they were excited to be involved in capturing this historical new breed of honeybees. It was something that none of them would ever forget. Even with all of the information that they had been given about the bees being killer bees, they were not really afraid of them, because they had all worked with millions of bees.

The doctor planned to capture the hive in several suitable boxes that he had brought with him from Washington. Because the hive was so massive he knew that the bees would be a little more crowded than normal, but it couldn't be helped. He didn't want to destroy any of the bees and he couldn't leave any of them behind. They had to all be taken together and he needed to capture every one of them alive.

The beekeepers quietly placed several large white sheets on the ground underneath where the swarm had settled. The boxes were put on the sheets and the massive swarm was then sprayed from the outside with a sugar solution. After waiting for a few seconds the beekeepers then vigorously shook the post and they tapped the side of the barn to shake the bees off onto the white sheets.

The bees clustered and then fell onto the white sheets and then quickly went into the dark entrance spaces in the openings of the boxes. An organized march ensued and the bees quietly marched into the boxes. The beekeepers used the suction pickup vacuum to transfer all of the remaining bees into the boxes to be taken in for observation. The expert beekeepers had collected all of the giant bees without a problem.

The observers watching from the military vehicle were absolutely in awe as they watched the entire procedure through the windows. Within minutes the bee collecting process was completed. You could hear everyone cheering and clapping from inside the vehicle once the beekeepers were done. The beekeepers had successfully gotten every one of the bees into several boxes.

The massive boxes were then put in the rear compartment of the military vehicles to be transferred back to the safety location. It had been a very heart-stopping ordeal, but the beekeeper's job had been a success and they were thrilled.

TWENTY-ONE

The Entomologist

All of the beekeepers talked incessantly on the way back to the safety location. They were so exhilarated after seeing the giant bees and actually capturing them without any problems. They could hardly wait to get back to the military facility and study the huge honeybees. They were all talking at once and laughing and joking and commenting on what a great opportunity it was for them to be there and see the wonderful giant bees. They commended Dr. Scans on his great ability to pull everything off without a hitch, but Dr. Scans said nothing.

Everyone in the military vehicle was talking except for the doctor from Washington. He just sat silently in his seat and stared at the floor. He seemed to just get angrier and angrier as he sat and listened to the constant chatter all around him. He acted like he wanted to cover his ears and block out the foolish gibberish, but of course he didn't. But he refused to talk to anyone. If anyone talked to him he never acknowledged them and he never even looked up. He was very distant and extremely odd.

He appeared to get more irritated the longer the journey took. But everyone else was so excited that they just kept on talking and ignoring him. They were all so energized that they barely noticed that the doctor was withdrawn and distant. He sat very rigid and if they had been paying any attention to him at all they would have been able to tell that he was just about ready to explode. He was definitely not a people person.

When the beekeepers and the bees returned to the safety location facility, the bees were put into an enclosed small laboratory room at the back of the facility. Of course the bees were left inside the boxes that they were captured in. The entomologist from Washington used state-of-the-art bee boxes with one side made of Plexiglas so that he could observe the bees as they were inside the containers.

The fanatical entomologist was absolutely obsessed with the gigantic honeybees. He had waited most of his lifetime to see honeybees this large, and he was completely besieged by what Mr. Faber had accomplished. He knew that there had to be a way to crossbreed the honeybee and he was euphoric that it had been accomplished by someone that had been on his team. He knew that in a round-about-way he had contributed to the conception of these wonderful creatures. He could only focus on the success of the giant crossbred bees; he was completely blind to anything else that had gone on. He did not even acknowledge the problems that the giant bees had caused; he could only see Mr. Faber's success.

Once the bee boxes were unloaded and placed in the small laboratory he could think of nothing else besides the giant bees. Dr. Scans sat down in front of the boxes to study them and he became oblivious of anyone else around him. He was not used to working with other people. The doctor had no tolerance for others; he had trained himself to block everything else out except for his work. He knew that if he ignored people long enough they would eventually just go away.

The other beekeepers were so good natured and excited about collecting the rare honeybees that they wanted to share their excitement with the doctor. He was the expert, he was the one who had done all of the research of the crossbreeding of the giant bees, so no matter how rude he was they tried everything to include him in the conversations. They kept asking him questions and trying to draw him into the discussion, but no matter what they did he would totally ignore them as if they were not even there.

They were really tying to work as a team, because they knew that they had a lot to accomplish and the doctor would again need their help. He could not do this alone. They thought if they just kept talking and asking him questions that eventually he would come around, but he never did. He refused to answer any questions that they asked him and instead he got more and more distant. It was very strange because he completely tuned every one of them out. He treated them so rudely that they began to think he couldn't even hear them talking to him.

Finally, the beekeepers gave up and left the doctor alone. The lab had a small restroom off to one side and so there was no reason for Dr. Scans to ever have to leave. When everyone else left the lab, the doctor locked himself inside and refused to leave and he wouldn't let anyone else back in to observe the bees.

Crossbreeding the giant honeybees had been his life's work and someone besides himself had finally accomplished it and he was captivated. He had dreamed about seeing the giant honeybees for a large portion of his lifetime. So, now that they had actually been created he would never again leave them or let anyone destroy them. Seeing his life's vision become real was absolutely breathtaking to him.

He knew that oftentimes in science you had to take misfortune with accomplishment. He had been told about the devastation and the deaths that the giant bees had caused, but he told himself that no one else understood them like he did. They had not researched the bees like he had and they were not professional scientists. They had not spent their entire lives trying desperately to develop the strong honeybees.

He knew that in the end his giant creation of honeybees would save the world. Honeybees would once again thrive and pollinate all plant life so the world would have plenty of food. He could barely breathe he was so energized about this world-changing discovery. One day everyone would know his name. He would be remembered in history as the scientist who rescued the giant honeybee; the scientist who saved the bees from annihilation.

Dr. Scans had been rude to the other beekeepers from the very beginning, but now that he had captured his prized bees, he no longer needed their assistance. He had no other use for them; so he was finished with the lowly beekeepers. He was the one that knew everything about the crossbreeding of honeybees and he didn't want to waste his time training everyone else.

The doctor acted like he was above all of the other people. He truly believed that they were his bees; it was his project because he had been working on the crossbreeding for many years. Now that the crossbreeding had been a success he didn't want something to happen to any of the bees. So, he locked the door to the lab and refused to talk to anybody. He wasn't going to let anything happen to his life's work.

The other beekeepers were a little frightened by him, because he acted so strange and out of control. He seemed oblivious to the fact that the bees had actually killed several animals and also his co-worker Franklin Faber, his wife Josephine and the wind turbine inspector. He honestly didn't care that the bees were so destructive. He could only see the perfection in the gigantic bees; he was completely blinded by Mr. Faber's success. You could tell that he planned to complete the work of Franklin Faber and he would guard the bees from anyone who tried to destroy them.

All he could see was the beauty of the giant honeybees. He had worked with millions of honeybees throughout his lifetime and he had never been afraid of them before, so he knew there was no reason to be afraid of them now.

He would guide them just as he had guided so many other hives. The crazy doctor was absolutely beaming inside because he knew that he would now be able to complete the book that he had been writing about saving the honeybee by crossbreeding. His work would go down in history as a renowned success.

The enlightened doctor sat down in front of the Plexiglas cage and started documenting their every movement. Within only a few short hours after his arrival he had page after page of documentation of the giant honeybee colony. He was utterly thrilled with his progress of the giant bees.

The doctor was so involved with his beehive that he refused to eat or even turn around when anyone came to the laboratory door. He acted as if he couldn't even hear them knocking. He didn't care if they were the military police, beekeepers or lab people in blue jumpsuits. He treated everyone the same. He completely ignored the reason that he had been brought to Idaho. His only focus now was to document and save the giant honeybees.

The military could have unlocked the lab door at any time and gotten into where the doctor was, but they decided just to leave him alone for awhile. He really wasn't hurting anyone, but the other beekeeper truly had planned on using his expertise for the dilemma with the wind turbines. The fanatical doctor ended up being more of a problem than a help.

Later that afternoon Dr. Keyes called everyone together in the auditorium, and of course the entomologist did not attend. But the three beekeepers were very open and honest. They apologized for the actions of Dr. Scans, because they had all figured out that Dr. Scans had no intentions of destroying any of the killer bees that remained inside of the wind turbines. They told the auditorium full of people that they would be forced to make all of the decisions on their own. They said that the doctor was so in awe of the massive bees that he refused to help them get rid of any of the giant honeybees. The beekeepers told the audience that they would have to take care of the problems at the wind turbines by themselves, because they would not get any help from the entomologist.

The beekeepers discussed how they could use 47 professional exterminators, one for each wind turbine at exactly the same time. They had started out with 48 turbines, but if turbine number seven was empty and all of the bees from that turbine were in the boxes down in the small lab that would still leave the 47 other turbines to worry about. They told the people that even with the bees from turbine number seven gone that they still were dealing with millions of bees that needed to be eliminated.

The beekeepers were concerned because now they were not even allowed to study the patterns of the giant honeybees that they had collected, because Dr. Scans would not allow anyone else in the laboratory to see them.

The beekeepers decided that after meeting Dr. Scans and observing his odd behavior they were now beginning to figure out the mindset of Mr. Faber. These scientists were fanatical about their crossbreeding of the giant honeybee. Apparently to them the success of the large bees was worth all of the destruction that had taken place. It was obvious that developing the giant bees was the most important thing in their life.

After talking to the audience and sharing their concerns about the situation, the beekeepers requested more time. They decided that they would spend the rest of the afternoon studying the large computer screens and watching the pictures of the wind turbines from the past several days.

They wanted to study the pictures of the turbines and their movements to get a better idea of exactly what was going on. The three beekeepers were not even friends, but they seemed to work well together. They had never seen each other until today. The only reason they were called in was because they were all three very knowledgeable about raising honeybees. But the bees in their hives at home were just normal honeybees. They were not aggressive or mean or oversized.

When the beekeepers asked for a few more hours to help them to prepare for the removal of the bees, the people at the head table looked at each other and frowned. They knew that they did not have a lot of time to wait. But as fearful as they all were they knew that it wasn't fair to ask the beekeepers to solve the messy situation without first going over the events of the past two weeks. The beekeepers wanted to watch the screens and determine what needed to be done.

It was decided that everyone would meet again at 7:30 in the morning, giving the beekeepers enough time to study the screens and decide the fate of the giant killer bees. The beekeepers also wanted to meet privately and share ideas. Up until now they had not really had an opportunity to talk confidentially amongst themselves.

They had all come to the Idaho location with the idea that they would assist the entomologist from Washington with whatever he needed them to do. Because they knew that he was the professional, he was the one with all of the expertise. He was the one that knew all about the giant crossbred bees.

But now they discovered that they would be forced to make all of the decisions on their own and they weren't sure what to do. Everything was different now, they were completely on their own to deal with the massive problem.

It was very overwhelming because they were dealing with millions of giant bees, many more than any of them had every dealt with before. And these bees were dangerous; they were nothing like anything the beekeepers had worked with previously. It was terrifying. Their excitement from working on the project with the doctor had now turned to panic.

As the beekeepers studied the screens from the past several days, they were absolutely horrified by all of the destruction that had taken place because of the giant colonies that were living in the huge wind turbines. The beekeepers soon realized that they had walked into a catastrophic situation when they came to Idaho to help. As they saw the screens of the destroyed properties and the blowing dirt, the massive wind gusts and the filth, they were absolutely overcome. All of the fallen trees, signs, glass and cluttered roads were just too much to digest in such a short period of time.

169

The old screens showed the firestorm where everything was burned beyond recognition. It showed the demolished homes, cars and businesses. The men read documents on the mangled deaths of the Faber's and the turbine inspector. They read through the reports of the dead horses, cows, the goat and then the five antelope. The beekeepers knew that they needed a little more time to grasp everything that had happened in the past few days before they could aid the community in solving this ruthless calamity.

There was a lot of pressure on the three beekeepers. They had never been involved in such a horrendous situation before and they had never dealt with any kinds of vicious bees. In fact they had always worked with honeybees as more of a hobby. They were very knowledgeable about bees, but of course this was the largest project that any of them had ever been involved in before.

One of the beekeepers was actually a teacher of apiculture and he communicated with beekeepers from all over the world, but he had never been involved with the African killer bees. The bees that the men were to dispose of had actually killed several animals and at least three people, so the beekeepers were not even sure that they wanted to be involved in this unspeakable situation. They were under no obligation to do this, but they could see that the people were desperate.

It was very confusing for the men; they knew they needed to help the community because they were in a hopeless situation, and no one else seemed to know what to do. But the beekeepers were just normal, humble people with wives and families. None of the men were what you would think of as heroes. The only thing that had brought them there in the first place was their knowledge of beehives.

TWENTY-TWO

The Answer

The beekeepers worked all through the night comparing their knowledge of bees and sharing ideas. They read through all of the accounts of the past few days and decided they would not quite be ready by 7:30 a.m. to make a decision on how to dispose of the bees in the wind turbines.

After reading all of the documentation of the disastrous things that had happened over the past couple of weeks they felt they needed time to process the information. Because they now realized that this was a much larger problem than just taking care of a few troublesome swarms.

This situation was more than just getting rid of a few beehives; this was a matter of life and death for this group of people. The bees had

171

caused momentous damage to homes, families, animals and the entire community. It could only get worse if the bees decide to leave the wind turbines and relocate in different locations. The killer bees could infiltrate the state of Idaho and eventually any of the surrounding states. So, the beekeepers had a lot of stressful decisions to make.

At 6:30 in the morning they notified Dr. Keyes that they were not yet prepared to meet and discuss the situation on how to handle the bees. The men stopped for a few minutes to eat the breakfast that had been brought in for them and then they went right back to work. They had the lab technician enlarge the screens and they studied the computer pictures section by section several different times.

They had studied the enlarged screens over and over again and found nothing. Finally as they broke the sections into smaller frames they noticed something odd that they had not noticed before. Something was dropping from the top of the turbines as the blades rapidly rotated around. They discovered tiny fragments that were continually falling from each wind turbine.

As they magnified the frames two or three more sizes they discovered it was actually small masses of bees dropping to the ground out of the sides of the wind turbines where the blade were attached. They couldn't believe that as many times as they had studied the screens that they had not noticed the masses falling out until now.

The lab people had been faithfully studying the wind turbines to make sure that the hives did not abscond, but they would never have noticed something as trivial and minute as a small cluster of bees dropping from the towers, a few clusters at a time.

When they magnified the screen even larger to see where the clusters of bees were falling from they discovered that the bees were somehow dying off and then just dropping all the way to the ground. They magnified the area around the base of the wind turbines and it was obvious that the bees were now dying off as quickly as they were reproducing, because there were thousands of dead bees around every turbine base. It was unbelievable that as many times as the beekeepers had studied the turbines on the screens that they had not noticed all of the dead bees piled up around each base before now.

As they studied wind turbine number seven they were shocked because it had double the amount of dead bees at its base. Mr. Mitchell, the first beekeeper said, "That may be why the bees in turbine number seven got stressed and absconded. The queen bee knew that her colony was dying faster than they were reproducing and she was relocating them to survive."

The beekeepers had the lab technician back up the screen to several days ago so that they could check and see just when the bees started to die off and fall to the ground. As they studied the first day when the lab had started tracking the turbines they could see nothing. The dead bees did not show up until a few days before the queen in turbine number seven absconded and relocated the hive. That was the same day that the other wind turbines began to lose bees from the blade area too.

As they studied the ground around each turbine they could tell that turbine numbers eighteen and twenty-six had accumulated a lot more bees than some of the other turbines had.

As they studied the masses falling from each turbine the second beekeeper, John Mouser said, "I have been interested in apiculture for over twenty-four years. Actually, even before that, I have been interested in bees since I was a young teenager. I now have friends from all over the world who are beekeepers." He continued talking as he stared at the screen, "I have written pamphlets on the art of beekeeping and I teach classes on apiculture and a couple of times a year I compare colony information with friends in England and Germany." Again without taking his eyes off of the screen he said, "The one thing that I have learned after all of my years of studying the honeybee is that there is a certain life cycle that each colony must go through."

He kept staring at the screen, "Of course the strand of honeybees that we are dealing with here is a freak of nature, because the bees have been crossbred so many times that their natural life cycle has been interrupted." He then jotted down some notes as he was talking and he said, "They have been crossbred many times to make them become larger and perhaps they mature at such a rapid rate that they may also run their life cycle much faster than is normal."

Mr. Mouser got an odd look on his face and continued on, "Let's say that the bees are running their life cycle so rapidly that they mature at several times the rate of a normal bee. Even as quickly as they are reproducing they are also dying off at a faster pace." He again got a strange look on his face, "I just thought of something, I want to check something on the screens."

He then went back to the giant screens to study the wind turbines again. Mr. Mouser said to the lab computer expert, "Would you please divide the screen into two sections." He looked at his watch and said, "It is morning and it is now 9:05 a.m. so from everything that we have been told the bees should be getting active and the wind turbines should be rapidly moving by now. I want to compare the current screen to the screen from four days ago."

Within a few seconds the split screen appeared on the walls. The screen from four days earlier showed the wind turbine blades rotating beyond recognition, but when they looked at the screen from today they could tell that the blades were slowing down.

Mr. Mouser then asked the lab technician, "Do you have an outside thermometer? I would like to see what the temperature is out near the wind turbines at the current time."

The lab technician smiled, tipped his head and chuckled as he said, "We are a climatology team from Penn State University; we were sent here to study the strange weather patterns. I can get you a second by second temperature schedule for every day since the day that we arrived and got set up."

Mr. Mouser laughed and patted the technician's shoulder that was sitting in the chair in front of him, "I'm working on the bees, I forgot for a minute why you guys came to Idaho in the first place." The lab tech nodded his head and chuckled again and then he instantly pulled up today's weather and a daily chart from the past seven days.

The beekeepers studied the weather chart and Mr. Mouser commented, "The outside temperature at the turbines is currently 49 degrees. Three days ago it was 71 degrees at this time in the morning. This is Idaho; when it gets summer-like weather too early, it will oftentimes cool off again before June. Before I moved to Arizona I lived here for many years and the weather can change 20 or 30 degrees in just a few days."

As they looked over the past seven day weather report they could tell that the days were getting cooler every day and bees do not like cold. Seven days ago the temperature was 80 degrees at this time in the morning.

The beekeepers went back to the split screen that showed the wind turbines today and the wind turbines from seven days ago when the team from Penn State had first arrived and they could tell that the rotation of the blades had slowed down considerably each day.

As they studied the current screens they saw that the bees were dropping from the turbines in giant masses. The colder weather was just too much for them and they had no one to protect them from the weather, because they had killed the one person who had protected them.

As they studied the screens, the lab technician pulled up the weather report for the next three days. It showed that dark clouds were rolling in and by later on this afternoon they expected lightening, thunderstorms and rain, perhaps even hail would pummel the entire region.

Mr. Mouser grinned as he stated, "It is very common to see hail this time of year if it gets hot too early. I forgot how unpredictable the weather can be in Idaho. By tomorrow the weather will only reach around 37 degrees and the summer-like weather will be over for awhile."

All three men just stood there and stared at the weather reports in disbelief. "Well this is Idaho and you know what they say, if you don't like the weather wait fifteen minutes," Mr. Mouser joked.

They continued to study the current screen and they watched in amazement because they could all tell that the blades on the wind turbines were slowing down considerably. Suddenly the blades on turbines eighteen and twenty six slowed to a normal rotating speed. The other lab technicians that were studying the individual turbines had not reported any of the hives absconding, so the beekeepers knew that the bees were still inside of the turbines.

As the beekeepers watched the screen, turbines four and twelve also slowed and turbine eight came to a complete halt and the blades did not move.

"What now?" The third beekeeper questioned. "What do we do if all of the wind turbines completely stop?"

As the men stood there puzzled staring at the screens, they received a note reporting that turbines four, twelve, eighteen and twenty-six had stopped functioning and they were shutting down. The note said that each turbine has a kill switch that automatically shuts down the wind turbines in the event of a problem.

"As if being invaded by millions of killer bees has not been a problem," the lab technician mockingly stated to the beekeepers as he studied the screens.

"We may not have to bring in all of the exterminators after all," Mr. Mouser excitedly stated. "The weather may take care of the bees for us. I think that they may be so crossbred that they aren't strong enough to survive the weather if it gets too cold. The weather seems to be bothering them even more than it does normal honeybees."

He shook his head back and forth and grinned as he stared at the screens as each turbine came to a halt, "Gentlemen, I think our bee problem has been solved."

TWENTY-THREE

An Act Of God

As the men stood there smiling and watching the screens trying to figure out what they needed to do next, a young lady in a blue jumpsuit brought a note to the three beekeepers. It said, "We have an emergency in the small lab where the entomologist is located with the bees. Could you please come at once?" It was signed from Dr. Keyes.

The beekeepers then followed the young woman back to the lab where the giant honeybees had been stored. As they arrived at the small laboratory they noticed several armed military guards standing outside the entrance. There were also people dressed in the blue lab jumpsuits standing near the doorway with Dr. Keyes and they were all looking in through the window.

As the beekeepers approached, Dr. Keyes turned to acknowledge them and he said, "We have a problem." As the beekeepers looked in the window they could see the mutilated body of the entomologist as he leaned over the open bee boxes. It was obvious that he had been stung to death by the killer bees because the door to the laboratory was still locked and no one had been in or out.

All of the bees had left the bee boxes and were swarmed around a large light fixture up near the center of the room. Apparently, the entomologist had trusted the bees and had let them loose and they attacked him. Already large masses of bees had begun to die off because they were unable to get close enough to the light to keep warm.

Mr. Mouser then exclaimed, "That's it. Turn on the air conditioning in that room and the bees will all die, just like they are dying out at the wind turbines."

Dr. Keyes looked shocked as he realized what the beekeeper had just told him. He excitedly questioned, "The bees in the wind turbines are dying?"

Mr. Mouser smiled and shook his head up and down as he answered, "Yes, I think all of our problems have been solved by an Act of God. The bees are actually dying and dropping out of the wind turbines in hoards. And I think that we can kill all of these bees too, if we can get it cold enough in the small laboratory so they can't survive. Bees hate cold weather and these giant bees seem to be even weaker than the normal honeybees are in the cold."

Dr. Keyes then eagerly told the lab technician to turn on the air conditioning in the small lab. They also turned off the light that the bees were all huddled around and within minutes the bees began to drop to the ground in big clumps. They would slowly flutter their wings trying desperately to communicate with each other for one last time and then it

179

was silent. There was no movement at all. Each giant honeybee was dead.

Everyone just stood there and gazed into the small lab room in amazement. Dr. Keyes looked at Mr. Mouser and said, "That was so easy."

"Bees can't take the cold weather. They need to be kept warm, clean and dry or they die. As we studied the screens we figured out that the weather is slowly taking care of the giant bee population out by the wind turbines, as we speak," Mr. Mouser happily stated.

"You mean we won't have to have every turbine of bees exterminated at the same time as you had suggested?" Dr. Keyes questioned.

"No, come with us and we'll fill you in on everything that we have discovered," Mr. Mouser told him.

As they walked back into the laboratory the technician handed them a new report stating that wind turbines number six, fourteen and thirty-eight had also gone into automatic shut down mode. As all of the men studied the screens Mr. Mouser said, "I'm thinking that because the weather is getting colder that the bees are dying off inside of the turbines and they are clogging up all of the gears. The masses of bees are no longer communicating and causing the elaborate vibration that Mr. Faber had written about in his journal."

Mr. Mouser went on with his theory, "I think that the millions of dead and dying bees are just packed inside of the turbines unable to get out or move. They are just smothering each other and so the wind turbines are automatically shutting down as they were designed to do when there is an emergency. The bees are clogging up the mechanisms and the wind turbines can no longer function."

Another note was brought to Dr. Keyes. He said, "Eight more turbines have stopped and have gone into emergency shut down mode. This is absolutely amazing, I am just stunned. I had no idea how we were ever going to take care of this horrible situation," he said shaking his head back and forth and smiling at the three beekeepers. "But with a blink of an eye it is taken care of."

"I know, I am amazed too, but tonight when the thunderstorm with hail and rain comes and the temperature drops that will finish off all of the rest of the bees," Mr. Mouser predicted. "And tomorrow my friends and I will go into the wind turbines dressed in our bee gear and start checking everything out."

He went on, "Someone will still have the problem of cleaning out the wind turbines to get them up and working again. I believe the owners of the wind turbines will most likely be in charge of that. Cleaning out all of the bees will be quite a massive undertaking, but at least they will not have to deal with the killing of all of the bees first. The bees should already be dead."

The wise beekeeper smiled at Dr. Keyes and said, "When we are done and all of the wind turbines are cleaned out and working again we can each go home knowing that we have done our jobs and we have gotten to the source of the mysterious winds of Tower County."

"I can't thank you enough," Dr. Keyes said, shaking each beekeeper's hand.

"We really didn't do much," Mr. Mouser said, "Actually, God took care of your situation with the bees in the wind turbines. He is the one who brought in the cold weather. All we did was study the bees to see what was going on. And of course we did help that crazy scientist from Washington get the bees that had gone over to Rockland, but that is about it."

181

"That is a lot," Dr. Keyes answered. "Would you be ready to make a statement this afternoon?"

"Sure, give us about an hour and we will be ready to talk to everyone. I think that by tomorrow after we get started in the turbines, your problems will all be settled," Mr. Mouser told him.

TWENTY-FOUR

The Dead Bees

Many of the people did not return to the auditorium to hear what the beekeepers had to say. They had heard that the bees would soon be taken care of and that's all that they cared about.

Darrell and I had been thrown into this mess by accident and we had come this far, so we were anxious to hear what the beekeepers had to say about this entire situation.

Mr. Mouser brought the audience up to speed on everything that had happened. He began by telling us again about the four beekeepers working together to collect all of the bees that had absconded and were discovered out in Rockland. He sadly told us that the bees had killed more animals on their way to the barn to relocate.

He told everyone exactly how they had sprayed the bees with sugar water and put sheets down and then shook the bees down onto the sheets. It was interesting how the bees just marched into the bee boxes and then they are contained. He made everything sound a lot easier than I'm sure it really was.

He solemnly told us about the entomologist locking himself in the room with all of the bees. He looked over at Dr. Keyes and Dr. Keyes nodded an o.k. so he sadly told us how the entomologist had lost his life by letting the bees out of the boxes inside the small laboratory.

We were relieved to hear that all of those bees were dead now too. He shared with the audience how they had turned on the air conditioning and all of the bees inside of the small laboratory dropped to the floor and died.

He assured everyone that the bees out in the wind turbines were also slowly dying off because of the colder weather. He said, "By tonight I think every one of the bees will be dead, because it will be too cold and wet for them to survive."

Mr. Mouser told us, "The honeybees were a new breed of bees and they appeared to be very hardy because they were so much larger than the normal honeybee. But they had been crossbred so many times that they were actually very fragile." He told us, "Although they had killed several people and several large animals they were not strong enough to survive the weather after it started getting colder." He continued on, "They were much larger than other honeybees and they appeared to be heartier, but we have discovered that they are actually a lot weaker. Being larger did not make them stronger."

All three beekeepers took turns sharing their thoughts. When they concluded with all of the information, Mr. Mouser got up to the microphone again and assured everyone, "By tomorrow this nightmare should all be over and all that will be left is the cleanup."

Dr. Keyes took the microphone once more and told the beekeepers, "I want to thank you again for all of your help." Then he turned to the people in the auditorium, "Tomorrow if all of the winds are gone, the military will go out and collect everyone that has been sent to other locations and bring them here. This is the largest facility and the government has decided that this would be a good place for the people of the community to meet up and get all of the families back together that have been separated for the past several days."

He continued, "Many of the people were taken to Pocatello, Twin Falls or Idaho Falls depending on what was the most convenient location at the time. If the bees and the winds are gone it will be time for everyone to meet in one place and make arrangements to go back into their homes. There will be a lot of cleanup to make the area livable once again. Many of the roads and properties have been totally destroyed. The winds have done so much massive destruction that much of the community is unrecognizable."

He told them "The entire region has been designated as a national disaster area by the federal government so the money will be distributed within the next few days so that people will be able to return to their homes and start rebuilding." He concluded, "Thank you so much for all of your help and patience. That concludes what I have for today."

Later on that evening Dr. Keyes began rounding up all of his documentation from the past week and a half to take back home with him. He knew that he would be leaving within the next few days and he was getting everything organized. He always had a lot of paperwork that needed to be done when he was finished with these emergency operations. Just as he was placing everything in special carrying boxes he received a note requesting that he return to the small laboratory where the entomologist had been killed.

When he got down to lab the cleanup people were just finishing up. They assured him that all of the bees had been disposed of and incinerated in a huge broiler. He was told that they had saved a few samples of the dead bees in a glass container to be used for future studies if they were ever necessary. They showed him the paperwork stating that the body of the man from Washington had been taken down to the morgue for evaluation.

It was government policy that the doctor in charge sign off that everything had been cleaned up and taken care of. They needed Dr. Keyes approval that everything was put back in order and sanitized. They were preparing to lock up the small lab room until it was needed again. It would not be used until the next time that the safety location was re-opened and it was required that it be left spotless.

As the doctor glanced around the room he realized that this small lab may not even be used again because it was just kind of an emergency over-flow lab, but it was a mandatory policy to always leave the labs spotless and clean when they closed them up. They needed Dr. Keyes signature before they could lock the room.

Dr. Keyes had signed the approval papers that the room looked orderly and clean and he was preparing to leave when he noticed a black notebook folded neatly on top of the desk where the entomologist had been sitting.

He glanced through the notebook and he was surprised to see that there were pages and pages of documentation written by the man from Washington. "He must have started documenting the bees as soon as he locked himself in here." Dr. Keyes quietly commented. He put the notebook under his arm and gave the o.k. to lock up the lab and then he headed back to his room.

As he passed the laboratory he told the lab techs that he was going to his room and he did not want to be disturbed. He then took a quick shower and went to bed. He could finally relax. It was the first time that he had slept all night since he had arrived at the Idaho safety location. The past week and a half had been a whirlwind of disasters and he was beyond exhausted. He fell asleep and didn't wake up until 7:38 the next morning.

In the morning he felt rested and relaxed; better than he had since his arrival. He was glad that this whole ordeal would finally be over. When he headed for breakfast he met up with the three beekeepers and they all sat down and ate breakfast together. The mood of every one of them was so much calmer, because their work was almost done.

As they were finishing their coffee, Dr. Keyes received a note stating that all of the remaining wind turbines had come to a halt. By afternoon the beekeepers knew that they would be able to safely enter all of the turbines and start checking them out before the cleanup crew could step in. They knew that they must finish their part of the inspection before the turbine specialists could began the horrendous job of cleaning out each turbine to get them working again.

The hail, rain and thunderstorms that had pulverized the towers during the night had now passed, but they had left the area around the wind turbines much cooler and damper. The colder weather had completed their mission, now it was time for the beekeepers and the cleanup committee to do theirs.

The beekeepers needed to check out every turbine before anyone else could enter into them. They were the only ones with the special safety beekeeping clothing in case they ran into any problem when they entered the turbines. They had to go first to make sure that it was safe for everyone else to go in.

The task of the turbine specialists would be absolutely overwhelming because there were so many turbines and each turbine was around 300 feet high. But they knew that somehow the wind turbines would have to be cleaned out so that they could be usable again. The turbine professionals could not get started until the beekeepers made sure that the cold weather had actually killed off all of the giant bees. If they found any bees still alive they would have to figure out a way to take care of them before anyone else could do their job.

* * * *

The three beekeepers and Dr. Keyes walked together down to the laboratory to check the screens to see what things looked like outside of the cavern. They were so pleased because every turbine was completely still and they could tell that the unnatural winds that had been caused by the bees had stopped completely.

The hail, heavy rain and thunder that had come in during the night had not only destroyed the bees, but it had helped to clean out the polluted air. It was very chilly because the weather had dropped considerably and everyone would need to wear a jacket, but the hillside around the wind turbines was once again sunny and clear. Only a few white fluffy clouds hovered over the destroyed region. As the men studied the turbines on the screen, it appeared that everything had returned to normal. The area gave no evidence of ever having any problems.

Dr. Keyes had hardly been out of the cavern for nine days. He had only been out once to go to the Faber's property. This was the longest time that he had ever been locked up inside of a safety location without being able to leave, so he decided to ride out to the turbine site with the beekeepers.

This past week and a half had been a very important part of his life and he knew that this horrendous experience would stay with him forever. He wanted to see firsthand what the wind turbines looked like up close. He had read so much about them, but he had never actually seen then up close before.

Dr. Keyes contacted Harold Pinson, the lead project manager for the Windsor Wind Farm and asked him to organize a team of turbine specialists to go out with them this afternoon. He wanted Mr. Pinson's team to go with them because they would be the ones that would be doing the cleanup of the wind turbines once the beekeepers gave the o.k.

At 1:00 P.M. all of the beekeepers, the wind turbine specialists, Mr. Pinson, Dr. Keyes and several military personal loaded into an army vehicle and headed out to the giant wind farm.

Dr. Keyes told us later that as they approached the first turbine where the two turbine inspectors had been attacked he instantly felt queasy and he had a hard time trying to catch his breath. His entire body broke out into a cold sweat. He was completely overcome with fear. He said that it hadn't occurred to him until they arrived at the wind turbines that maybe some of the killer bees were still alive. He worried that possibly only a large portion of the bees had died, but a few of them could have survived. He rationalized that if there were only a handful of live bees they would not be able to make the wind turbines go around, but they could easily kill every one of the men in his group.

189

As they pulled up and stopped at the first turbine the beekeepers instructed everyone to stay inside of the military vehicle until they had time to check the turbines out. Mr. Pinson gave them a key to unlock the door at the bottom of the giant turbine. Everyone that remained inside the military vehicle stared intently out the front window watching and waiting to see what the beekeepers would find.

The three beekeepers got out of the vehicle and took turns taping each other's sleeves and pant legs. They were just being extra cautious in case they encountered live bees. They did not want to take a chance on any surprises if for some reason some of the bees had been protected more than others and they had survived through the cold and wet night. When they had all of their gear securely in place they headed over to the door at the bottom of turbine number one.

They nervously walked up the steps to put the key into the solid metal door when a glob of dead bees hit Mr. Mouser on the top of his hat. All three men jumped back and let out a quick yell before they realized what had happened. As they studied the ground around turbine one they noticed thousands and thousands of dead bees piled haphazardly everywhere around the base.

They cautiously started for the door again, but before they could get to the knob another blob of dead bees plopped to the ground right in front of them. But this time they ignored the interruption and they continued to walk on up the steps to the door. As they put the key into the door they discovered that the lock would not turn. Something inside of the turbine was jamming the lock and preventing the key from going in.

Mr. Mouser walked back to the military vehicle and got a screw driver to try to clear out the keyhole. When he returned with the screw driver and dug out the entrance, the key finally went in and he took a deep breath and turned the key in the lock. As the large metal door flew open a whoosh of dead bees streamed out and covered the ground around the steps and the entire base of wind turbine number one. The weight of the massive hive continued to flow out the door until it got a blockage about 50 feet up and clogged the tower inside and the bees stopped pouring out.

As the beekeepers pushed the bees aside to get a look inside of the turbines they were shocked at the vastness of the interior of the turbine. As they looked up through the center they could spot globs of honeycomb and dead bees attached at several different locations all the way up as far as they could see. But they could not see any live bees. Every cluster that they found was definitely dead and there was no noise of any kind. There was no movement or any sound of buzzing. The wind turbines had automatically shut off and everything was completely silent even the soft humming of the rotating blades had become completely still.

The beekeepers walked back over to the military vehicle and told the men inside that all of the bees that they had found were dead. They got back into the vehicle and drove down to the next turbine. They drove from one turbine to another, but never found any live bees in any of the giant turbines.

There were dead bees covering the ground around every turbine, but there was no movement at all.

After checking out all 48 turbines the beekeepers concluded that every one of the giant honeybees had died. They found no signs of movement anywhere on the entire wind farm. There were thousands of bees packed into each wind mill and as many scattered all around the bottom of the each turbine, but they were all dead. The cleanup of the turbines would be absolutely brutal because the bees had made such a huge mess, but since the beekeepers found no live bees, the cleanup could begin immediately.

After going through every turbine the men drove back to the first turbines and everyone cautiously got out of the vehicle. The beekeepers wanted the turbine specialists to see exactly what they were dealing with. They wanted them to see for themselves what they needed to do to clean up and restore the wind turbines back to the way that they were.

Dr. Keyes told us that when he finally got the opportunity to get out of the vehicle and stand at the foot of turbine number one he could not believe how ominous it was. As he stood near the bottom of the turbine and stared up towards the blades he couldn't even see the top of the wind turbine because it was so gigantic.

He told us that looking down the rows of perfectly placed wind turbines out at the wind farm was a sight to behold. He was so intimidated by the size of the turbines that he could not help but just stand and stare. They were so enormous that it was absolutely mind-boggling. He was so impressed by the giants that he got out his phone and took several pictures to send home to his family. It was a spectacular sight that he was sure that he would never have the opportunity to ever see again in his lifetime.

As Dr. Keyes took pictures of the turbines, one of the specialists from Mr. Pinson's team went inside of turbine number one and began to climb up the ladder that was located up the center of the tower. Climbing up through the wind turbine was a task that he had done many times before. But this time as he climbed up he had to push aside hoards of dead bees and just let them drop to the bottom the giant tower. The tower was in total mayhem. It was cluttered with honeycombs and globs of lifeless bees.

When he approached the top he was completely blocked off from getting through by huge honeycombs and the massive bee colony. Apparently, this is where the main colony of bees had first swarmed and located. He could tell that the bees had originally entered through the top of the turbine and swarmed around the blade area. It was just as the specialists had guessed, because this was where most of the masses were located. He dug and moved globs of bees and honeycombs around until he could see a slight hole only large enough to see through towards the top of the turbine.

It was a little creepy climbing up the center of the turbine with all of the clusters of giant dead bees, but he had a job to do and he was the lead turbine specialist, so it was up to him to get the job done. He knew that they would need something to clean off the gooey honeycombs and knock down all the hoards of clumped bees. It would take several turbine workers to get all of the towers working again, but at least now they had a better idea as to what needed to be done to get everything back to normal.

Mr. Pinson and the lead specialists decided to return to the safety location and get their team organized to begin cleanup on the turbines right away. They knew that the sooner they got started the sooner they could get everything working again. They would need some sort of portable incinerator to dispose of all of the bees after they were knocked to the base or to the ground.

All of the men got back into the military vehicle to return to the safety facility. Everyone felt confident that the torment of the killer bees would soon be behind them and the community could get their lives back together.

TWENTY-FIVE

Crisis

By the time that Dr. Keyes and his team returned to the safety facility, a lot of the other evacuees from other locations had been brought in. Many of the people that had been evacuated to Pocatello, Twin Falls and Idaho Falls had already been brought over to this location to meet up with their families.

Once again Dr. Keyes met with everyone in the large conference room and brought us all up to date on everything that had been happening at the wind turbines. He told us about the beekeepers checking out all of the towers and finding all of the bees dead. He assured everyone that the day of the mysterious winds was now over and it wouldn't be long before everyone could return to their homes.

We knew that we would soon be leaving, but first we had to find our friends. They had not been brought in on any of the trucks so far, but we decided to go stand down by the truck entrance for the next truck load to arrive.

After everyone was dismissed we stood up to leave the auditorium, but before we could get away we were approached by Dr. Keyes. He asked if he could talk with us for a few minutes. He shared with us some of the fears that he had been having in the past few days. He also told me, "I want to thank you personally for noticing the dark cloud of bees when you first came to this facility. If you had not told us about the dark clouds, we would have never been able to figure out what was causing the horrendous winds that were destroying the area."

He said, "We could figure out that the wind was only on the front side of the wind turbines, but no one had been able to figure out why. I don't know how we could have ever figured out that something inside of the turbines was creating the destructive winds. We would have never guessed that the wind turbines had been inundated with giant crossbred bees. Even saying that out loud sounds bizarre. So thank you again for noticing something that none of the rest of us had noticed."

I smiled and said, "Thank you, but all I did was see a dark cloud mass in the sky when I was looking through the binoculars out at the safe-haven location. We are just glad that this is almost over and you could find a solution to this terrible situation. It has been quite an adventure for all of us, but we will be glad when we can find our friends and head back to Boise. We are hoping that our friends will be in the next military group that comes in because we haven't been able to find them yet."

My husband added, "I have never seen a wind turbine up close and I hear that they are quite intimidating. What did you think when you were out there today?"

Dr. Keyes then set all of his papers down on a chair and got out his phone to show us the pictures that he had taken earlier in the day. We were in awe just as he had been. The pictures on his phone were clear and precise and we just stared in disbelief at how enormous each tower looked. Wind turbines really are amazing.

As we were looking at the phone pictures, someone in blue lab clothes interrupted Dr. Keyes and he once again had to leave.

We decided to head down to the military entrance to try to find our friends. I turned to get my purse and realized that Dr. Keyes had left his papers and a notebook on the chair as he was showing us the turbine pictures on his phone. I looked around the room, but he was gone. I picked up the papers and planned to give them to him later. He was such a nice man; he was the kind of person that we would choose as a friend.

We walked down to the military entrance, but we were told that no other vehicles would be coming in with people for several hours. So, we returned to our room to wait until our friends would arrive at the safety location. As we walked through the large waiting room we saw families reuniting and each chair and couch was crammed with many new faces that we had not seen before.

We got to our room at the end of the hall and decided to rest for an hour or so before going back to wait for the next military vehicle. We had nothing else to do, so my husband sat down on his bed and decided to sleep for awhile.

As I climbed to my top bunk I accidentally dropped the papers and the black notebook that belonged to Dr. Keyes. As I picked up his papers I noticed a couple of pages of scribbled notes that he had read when he talked to all of us in the auditorium. But the notebook was written in someone else's handwriting so it caught my attention. It fell

196

open to the third page so I quickly read just the first two lines before I knew that it was written by the entomologists from Washington.

I skimmed over the page and I could tell that the entomologist was writing notes about the giant honeybees that he had collected out at the Rockland farm area. Everything he wrote showed how much he adored the giant killer bees. He cared nothing about the danger or extreme damage that the bees had done. He only saw their uniqueness and their beauty.

As I read a few more lines I jumped down from the bunk and told my husband, "We've got to go find Dr. Keyes." And then I headed out the door with my sleepy husband close behind me.

We found Dr. Keyes down in the laboratory and we sent him a message that we needed to meet with him alone immediately. He got the note and took us in his office.

I handed him the black notebook and asked him if he had read through it? He said, "No, I had it with me and I had planned to look it over, but I couldn't remember where I had put it down."

I shuddered as I handed it to him, "I think you'd better read it. I picked it up for you when you left it on the chair while you were showing us the wind farm pictures. I'm sorry, I didn't intend to read any of it and actually I just read a few lines on the third page, but trust me that was enough."

Dr. Keyes sat down at his desk and began to read through the black notebook. The first page that he had glanced at before was just notes about the creation of the giant bees, but as he read the next two pages he looked up at me and covered his face and paled, "Oh no, what has this crazy scientist done to us?"

He instantly went to his door and requested that Dr. Tomlin gather some of the other people on his team and come to his office immediately. After everyone arrived in his office the doctor told them that he was going to read the black notebook that had been left behind by the entomologist from Washington.

He started with page 3: The entomologist wrote, "The giant honeybee is the greatest creation that has ever been made. I will do anything to save it. I only wish that I had my protective bee clothing because I am going to open the bee boxes and save the queen, several drones and many of the worker bees. I know that I am the only one that can save this wonderful crossbred creation, and I have to do it today before it is too late."

The scientist continued, "I see the wonder in this beautiful hive, because I have spent years of research trying to create it, but everyone else can only see its destruction. My plan is to save part of the hive today before any of the lab people can get to them. I discovered a Pneumatic tube transfer system in the back of the laboratory. After transporting the queen and some of the drones and worker bees to a safe location I will be able to collect them later and take them back to Washington with me where they will be safe. My master honeybee creation will live on and no one will ever be able to stop me. After I transfer the bees I will casually leave the laboratory and not a soul will ever suspect what I have done.

There are so many bees in this massive hive that not even the beekeepers will notice that the queen and some of the other bees are gone. I will leave a good portion of the drones and worker bees in the bee boxes and they will never notice that they have been tricked and that I have already saved the queen."

Dr. Keyes stated that the next few lines are almost illegible, but it says, "I have safely transported the queen and several of her workers, but I have made the drones angry and I have had to endure quite of few bites. I cannot get the bee boxes closed back up because my hands are bleeding and my eyes will soon be swollen shut. I have never seen such vicious creatures before in my life. What have I done? These truly are killer beeeeees..."

Dr. Keyes sorrowfully looked up, "That is where the doctor's notes end." He shook his head back and forth, "Does anyone know anything about this Pneumatic transfer tube that he is talking about?"

Every one in the room just sat silent for a few moments. They were all stunned. Dr. Tomlin finally spoke, "They are the kind of tubes that you use at a bank to transfer money from your car to the bank teller. I've used them before in other laboratories, but I didn't realize there was even a transfer tube system here in the cavern, but it makes sense because everything in the cave is so spread out."

"How would we know where the doctor had sent the tube?" Dr. Keyes questioned.

"I'm not sure." Dr. Tomlin stood up and said, "Let me see if I can find someone that knows anything about where the transfer tube would actually go."

While she was gone Dr. Keyes sent someone down to get the three beekeepers. He wanted them to know that we may still have a problem. He requested that they each bring their protective bee gear. As soon as the beekeepers got the message they grabbed their gear and came at once.

Just as the beekeepers arrived Dr. Tomlin returned with the computer maintenance man. He was in charge of all of the computers and equipment in the entire safety location.

Dr. Keyes sadly told the beekeepers and the head maintenance man about the frightening situation that they were in with the transported bees. Every one of us then got up and followed the maintenance man down the hall to the small lab where the entomologist had been killed by the bees. He unlocked the door and turned on the lights and then he walked over to a small casing area where the Pneumatic transfer tube was located.

After looking everything over he stated that the tube that was used to transfer the bees did not return because the casing was empty. He said that it was the state of the art transfer tube and he could easily track where the tube had gone. He used a special walkie-talkie device that could be used inside of the cave to call the controller to track where the tube had ended up. Within seconds the report came back stating that the tube had been transferred to the back door area at the outside military guard location.

The controller also told him, "My records state that the tube transfer has never been used before. No one ever uses that lab, it is just an overflow and it is rarely needed. So, there has never been anything sent out of there before now."

As we were leaving the small laboratory a lady in a blue jumpsuit arrived carrying a glass container with a tray filled with several of the dead bees. She wanted to show the doctor the specimen tray that she had saved. She was showing him the bees that she had collected while she was cleaning up the lab and preparing to lock it up.

Dr. Keyes inspected the container of bees for a second and before handing it back to the lady to store away, he showed the container to all of us. He wanted every one of us to see what the giant honeybees looked like.

They were unreal. They looked to be about two inches long and as wide around as a tube of lipstick. They were a beautiful golden-brown color that kind of glistened as the opaque wings caught the reflections from the laboratory light fixtures and kind of leaped off in the air as the glass case changed positions. I stared in disbelief at the enormity of the giant creatures. They were unlike anything I had ever seen before. No wonder the entomologist was so in awe of them. It was hard to comprehend that these dazzling creatures had been so caustic.

As the lady took the container of bees away, the rest of us followed the maintenance man down a long hallway and through a dark back stairway. Apparently, we were going down some sort of private back access. We walked down several steps before coming to a large landing where there were several huge military vehicles parked.

The beekeepers got dressed in their protective gear and requested that everyone please stand back while they check out the area where the maintenance man told them to go. The brave beekeepers crept over to investigate the place where the giant bees were supposed to have gone. The rest of us stood back out of their way until they were done checking the area.

When they got to where the tube was supposed to be, they found the casing was empty. Someone had already retrieved the tube and the tube and the bees were gone. We knew that the entomologist had never left the lab so we had no idea who would have gotten the bees.

The maintenance man radioed back to the controller to make sure that this was the correct location where the scientist had transferred the bees. He sadly discovered that this was definitely where the computer had tracked the Pneumatic tube transfer, but the bees were gone. No one had any idea what had happened to them and there was nothing that any of us could do about them now.

Dr. Keyes solemnly thanked everyone for their help and then we walked back to the main section of the building, feeling more baffled than we had before. On the way back the beekeepers told us that they didn't think that the bees could survive for long being trapped inside of a plastic tube.

It had been almost twenty-four hours since they had found the entomologist dead in the small laboratory, so they felt that the bees that the entomologist had transferred were all dead too. But there was no way for anyone to know for sure.

TWENTY-SIX

Our Friends Arrive

After returning to the main location we all went our separate ways. Darrell and I headed for the military entrance to wait for the next load of people to come in. Hopefully our friends would be arriving soon. With everything else that was going on we were getting more anxious to find our friends and get out of there.

As we sat on the bench waiting for the transports to come in, I began feeling very unsettled and I almost wished that I hadn't found the scientist's black notebook. We were probably all better off just thinking that the killer bees had all been destroyed. Now we are not sure where the bees ended up and if they are dead or alive.

My cluttered thoughts were interrupted by the sounds of the huge military transfer vehicles arriving with more people. I stood up to get a clearer view of the people entering the facility and some of the first people off of the transport were our good friends Suzanne and Gene.

Everyone coming into the safety location looked dazed and confused. They all acted like they had no idea where they were being dropped off. These poor people had been through so much and they probably just wanted to go home.

"Suzanne," I hollered. "Over here." I had forgotten for a minute that our friends did not even know that we had come to rescue them. We had no way to communicate and although we had been here for several days, they wouldn't expect to see us here.

We pushed our way through the crowd until we could get to where they were standing. "What are you guys doing here?" Suzanne questioned throwing her arms around my shoulders.

"Actually, we came to rescue you guys probably five days ago," I said with one arm around her waist. "But it has taken us all this time to find you."

After Gene and Darrell shook hands and bear hugged, we headed for the reservation area to find them a room. After getting them a room by us, we went to the cafeteria and sat down to have a cup of coffee.

As soon as we found a table Suzanne began telling us everything that had happened to them. "You cannot even imagine the ordeal that we have been through in the past week," Suzanne said trying to bring us up to date.

I looked at Darrell and smiled, but said nothing. "Yeah, we probably could imagine," I said inside of my head.

Suzanne continued to tell us how they had been rescued about an hour after we talked on the phone last week. She said, "The military and the police department had gone around and made everyone evacuate. They said that the whole area was unsafe for anyone to stay in their houses. They told us that they were taking us all to a safety location."

She rubbed her hands across her face before going on, "The police and military were still rescuing people when they ran out of time and the sun came up. Our group was traveling in a giant military transport vehicle when the wind started to blow and it blew a huge tree into a gas truck and started a horrible fire. The entire area all around us went up in flames. It was just unbelievable. We were scared to death."

She went on, "The transport vehicle that we were riding in got trapped in the fire and we had to quickly trade to a different truck or we would have burned up in the fire just like the transport truck did."

She covered her face with her hands before going on, "You can't even imagine how terrifying it was moving all of those people from one truck to the other. We all thought we were going to die. We had to smash every one of us into one vehicle. Those military vehicles are huge, but we still had to sit on top of each other to get everyone into one truck." She shook her head back and forth and kind of shivered, "All we cared about was getting out of there."

Suzanne paused for a second, "We were already having difficulty breathing before everyone had to smash altogether, because the air was so polluted. People were coughing and choking and wheezing. It was awful because the air was so heavy and contaminated that we could barely see."

"Everyone was so scared, but it was amazing because some of the local men were picking people up and carrying them on their shoulders to get them to the other transport truck. The whole situation was just incredible." She said squeezing my hand.

"Since we were trapped on the other side of town they took our group of people into Pocatello instead of bringing us out here like they had planned. So, we have been in a gym in Pocatello for the past week," Suzanne went on. "But why are you guys here?"

"When we couldn't reach you on the phone, we got in the car and came over to bring you home with us, we came to rescue you." I answered. I smiled, "Actually, it is kind of long story, but anyway we ended up here waiting until we could find you. We were hoping that you would eventually come here."

"Did you know that they think all of this started because of some giant bees?" Suzanne commented. "Can you believe that?" She shook her head back and forth and said, "We had to drive through town to get here and all of the damage is just mind-boggling. I can't quite see how bees could have done that much destruction. I can't imagine why they are blaming all of this on giant bees. How could bees make the wind blow so violently?" she questioned.

I just smiled because as I listened to her talk I realized that I knew way more than I should know. Probably more than any of the people of the community will ever be told. We just happened to get thrown into this horrible situation by accident. We were just innocently coming to rescue our friends and we got trapped here.

It was never our intention to get so involved, so as I listened to her talk, I wondered if we would ever tell our close friends the whole truth of the past week; probably not. I can't see that telling the horrible things that have happened could ever benefit anyone. Only a handful of us know the entire truth about the mysterious winds, and I'm sure that Darrell would agree it is not our place to tell anyone. We are just a couple of innocent bystanders that were in the right place at the right time otherwise we too would just be reading about the mysterious winds in the newspaper.

As we sat there in the bright cafeteria drinking coffee and just visiting and trying to calm our nerves, a strong voice came over the loud speaker requesting that everyone meet up in the conference room in fifteen minutes.

We finished our coffee and showed our friends the way to the conference room. There were people everywhere. Many of the new people were standing around the outside of the chairs looking a little lost and out of place. There were hundreds of new faces in the room; farmers, people sitting alone, large families, wealthy merchants, police, and firemen. I'm sure the entire community was crammed into this one giant space.

Our chairs up front sat empty as well as two of the other chairs next to them, so Darrell and I led our friends down to the front area to take our usual places. Some of the people that we had seen at several of the other meetings nodded or waved a quick hello.

The three beekeepers were sitting off to our left and they too gave a friendly wave. Our good friend Dr. Keyes smiled and nodded his head towards us as we took our seats and sat down. I smiled back at him and nodded hello. We had all been through a lot together in the past week, things that only we can share with each other and will most likely never share with anyone else.

Suzanne leaned over to me and said, "Who is that? How do you guys know all of these people?"

"The man up front is the lead meteorological scientist for the wind project here at the safety location. He was sent here to get to the source of the vicious wind problems. And many of the other people we have just seen quite a few times throughout the week as we were here waiting to find you guys," I answered honestly.

Several new people that had just come to the safety location stood up and spoke. They could have been ministers, the town council, important business owners, I'm not sure exactly who they were, but the local people seemed to know them. The speakers encouraged the citizens of the community to once again work jointly to help put their community back together again.

Soon a government man in a black suit told the audience that the authorities would be distributing money within the next few days for the people to begin rebuilding. The entire county was considered a national disaster area and the government had designated several million dollars to help clean up the community.

A prominent looking man that I had never seen before stood up and talked. I could tell that the people of the area knew him and he encouraged everyone by promising them that they would be able to return to their homes in a day or so. The man told the people of his town that they had a lot of work to do, but he stressed that the community was strong. He eagerly encouraged them that they had done it before and if they all helped, he knew that they could again rebuild their town back to the way that it was. After he spoke the whole room seemed more upbeat and energized.

Dr. Keyes then stood up and introduced himself to all of the new people in the audience. He told them, "I have been informed that because of the terrible air pollution throughout the valley that the health advisors would like you to wait at least another 24 hours before allowing anyone back onto their properties. The rain that came in a couple of days ago helped to clear out some of the pollution, but the air quality has been so serious that they do not want all of you exposed to any more contamination than you need to be."

TWENTY-SEVEN

The Community

On our last night at the safety location we ate dinner with Suzanne and Gene, and then we decided that we would go with them the next day to check out the damage of their property before we headed home. We never told our friends that we had already been to their house when we first came into town. The less we talked about what we had done when we first arrived, the less confusion there seemed to be and the fewer questions we had to answer.

It had been a very interesting week, but Darrell and I were both anxious to head home. Suzanne and Gene would not be going with us. They planned to stay here and rebuild their property. Even with everything that has happened they still loved living in Tower County and they had no plans to move back to Boise.

At least we had a couple of days to visit with our friends and we knew that they were safe and all right. The crisis in the county was over and now it was time for everyone to rebuild. We knew that by the time we headed home we would feel much better about our good friends. Our home was in Boise and we realized their home was here. We planned to come back in a couple of months when the town was a little more back in order.

We waited with our friends at the front entrance for the transfer vehicles to arrive to take them home. The military told everyone that had come in on a military vehicle that they had to also be taken out in a military vehicle. They wanted to make sure that everyone was accounted for. So, we waited with them until they were loaded in the transfer truck with all of their neighbors before we headed to our car.

We had plenty of time because we knew that it would take the trucks much longer to get to Suzanne and Gene's house than it would for us. The transfer trucks had to distribute every one of the people and their families to their homes and they had several stops to make before they reached our friends house. It would not take us as long to get to their house even if we had to drive a lot slower on the old abandoned desert road that we had come in on.

After getting our friends on the transfer truck we headed for our car. As we climbed the steep spiral staircase to leave I felt a little sadness. We had said our goodbyes to Dr. Keyes, Dr. Tomlin, Mr. Pinson and the three beekeepers. It always amazes me how quickly people can walk into your life and then stay a part of your memories forever. The one lesson that I have learned from all of this is that there are good people everywhere. All you have to do is look. We made some wonderful new friendships through this horrendous disaster, but now every one of us is weary and ready to go home.

Driving out through the desert to find the highway was much simpler without the dust, debris and the horrific winds. We bumped and bounced as we cautiously drove over the pitted dirt road that we had so violently driven in on only a few short days earlier.

It was slow and tedious traveling, but we finally arrived at the rubbish covered highway. Even in the daylight it was hard to tell where the highway had been and where it was now eroded away. We turned onto the main road and headed towards Suzanne and Gene's house where we planned to meet up with them after the military truck dropped them off.

We were there waiting for them when they returned home to their unbelievably devastated property. They could barely recognize their beautiful little farm with so much destruction. We helped Gene move garbage away from their roof, driveway and car as Suzanne hysterically walked around and cried. Everything was destroyed.

The huge trees had demolished the roof and half of the front room. Our friends had many broken windows and much of the siding had disappeared off of their house. We could see water damage from the heavy hail and rain that had come in a couple of nights ago and had gone right into the house because of the missing ceiling and roof.

It would take weeks to get the huge tree branches cut up and hauled away. Their entire yard was covered in enormous old toppled trees. Darrell and I tried to move some of the smaller branches over to the side of the driveway so that they would be able to get their car out when they needed too.

We all moved things around for several hours trying to make a small dent in the colossal mess that our good friends had come home to. When we felt like we had done as much as we possibly could we decided to head home.

Before we left we helped our friends climb down inside of their basement to check it out and to make sure that they would have a place to sleep later on that night. The weather was a little cool, but the cellar was still pretty usable. It had been protected and it had minimal destruction. They had endured a lot of damage, but at least the horrible winds were gone and they were home on their property and ready to rebuild.

A truck had stopped by earlier with several gallons of water and the authorities had told everyone that the county was going to send people around within the next few days to help with the fallen trees and broken windows.

We all prayed together and then we sadly hugged our friends, said goodbye and got into our car and drove away. It would take us quite awhile to get back to where the safe-haven location had been set up and where the roads were not destroyed. All of the streets close to town were damaged and we knew that we would have to literally crawl over a lot of the wreckage and debris before we could reach the highway.

I sobbed as we left our friend's demolished house and headed home. We carefully drove back through the garbage, fallen trees, and the collapsed properties. All along the way we saw people working together to put things back to the way they were before the winds interrupted their lives.

Already large groups of the local citizens were out picking up trash and rubbish off of the highway so that people could drive through. As we went past, everyone smiled and waved as if we too belonged to this amazing group of neighbors. Well, perhaps we did...at least we did for the past several days.

It was heartwarming to watch the community moving forward, they did not pause for one day. They began rebuilding as soon as the military vehicles brought them back home.

As we drove through town I gazed out the window in amazement. No wonder our friends loved this small community so much. Every one of us wants a place to belong, a place of purpose, a place to be involved and a place where every person can bond together as one. A community is just an ordinary group of people standing united to make up an army that can overcome anything.

By the time we reached the highway we had left all of the people behind. We could not believe the total annihilation that was everywhere; the trash, the garbage, and the filth. Every place that we looked was destroyed. It would take months to get this region back to some sort of normalcy.

We crept along the highway until we passed the old road that led up to the safety location. We would never again look at an old abandoned dirt road in the same way; especially one that heads out to the desert and goes into the side of a mountain. From now on we will always wonder where each road leads.

It wasn't long before we got to the area that had not been touched by the violent winds. The road was once again just a regular highway. My husband picked up speed and we were on our way home.

As we approached the area that had been set up as the safe-haven location we noticed that everyone was gone. It had served its purpose and it was no longer needed. I couldn't help but get a strange feeling in the pit of my stomach as I glanced over at the magnificent giant wind turbines as we passed by. For one quick second I feared seeing a dark black cloud swiftly floating through the sky, but luckily I saw nothing.

214

I have always enjoyed the beauty of that area with the canyon, the cliffs and the Snake River. Today the road was deserted. We traveled alone in and out of the rolling canyon because there was not one other car, pickup or delivery van anywhere. The road had been blocked off for so many days that the people had started going other directions, but they would soon be back.

We met no other cars on the road until we got to the interstate turn off and headed for Burley. The freeway traffic was constant and we knew that we were finally getting to civilization and that our world too would soon get back to normal.

TWENTY-EIGHT

Home Sweet Home

We were within 45 miles of our house when we realized that we had not eaten since breakfast at the safety location. We were both starved so we decided to stop in Mountain Home and have dinner before we drove on into Boise.

If we got dinner out of the way before we got into town then we wouldn't have to worry about fixing anything and we could get a few things done when we got home. We had been gone for over a week and there were a lot of things that had been neglected around our house.

We pulled into a small restaurant out on the outskirts of town. Darrell checked our gas gage and decided we still had plenty of gas to get all of the way home. We hadn't bought gas since we bought it in

Burley over a week ago. Luckily, our Chrysler is really good on gas especially on the freeway.

We pulled into a parking space and then we stood up and stretched because we had been sitting in the car for hours. It had not been a normal kind of trip; all day long our travels had been very stressful and I was more than happy to stand up.

After we had dinner we headed back out to the car to go home. As I reached for the car door I could hear several people shouting and squealing over on the other side of the building. Everyone was talking at once and the more the people talked the larger the crowd gathered around to see what all of the commotion was about.

Darrell and I were very tired and we decided to just ignore the ruckus and get into our car and leave. All that we cared about was going home. As I reached for the door again I overheard a man shout, "That is the largest bee that I have ever seen in my life."

A lady hysterically screamed, "Is it dead? Where do you think it came from? It is so huge. I am terrified of bees." The lady just kept screaming.

Darrell and I instantly looked at each other and I whispered, "Oh, No" We both closed the car doors and slowly walked over to where all of the people were jabbering at the same time.

There were probably nine or ten people standing there and all of them were shouting and talking about the giant honeybee that the truck driver was holding in a napkin in his hand. "Where did you get that?" I discreetly asked the driver.

"I just found it on the windowsill of the restaurant right over near the front door," the man stated proudly. "I have never seen a bee this big before in my life. I'm going to take it home to show it to my kids. I wonder what kind it is."

217

"Well, let's hope it's not a killer bee," another man said jokingly as all of the people laughed at once.

Darrell and I looked around the flowerbeds and we searched the area around the windowsill, but we could not see any other bees, so we got back into our car and headed home. We felt discouraged because we now knew that somehow at least one of the bees had made it all the way to Mountain Home.

We arrived at our house about 6:30 p.m. We were tired, exhausted and glad to be home. I fixed us some coffee and unloaded the car as Darrell went out and mowed the front yard. The past week had been very challenging so we spent the rest of the evening just trying to unwind.

I made a few phone calls to let all of our kids know that we were back home safely and then we watched the channel 7 news before going to bed. The evening news showed a small caption of the destruction in Tower County and then it told how all of the people had been returned to their homes. The news did not mention anything about the bees. It only told that the mysterious winds were now over and the county would soon be back to normal.

The next day when I talked to my three youngest grandkids on the phone we decided to have a sleepover. We had not seen anyone for over a week and we loved having our grandkids come and play.

Grandpa and I put up a tent in the family room so that the kids could have a camp out...inside. When they slept in the tent I always slept in a recliner chair beside them, so they were not left out in the family room all alone. As a Grandma I have learned to sleep almost anywhere.

I went to the store and got snacks, some ingredients to make cookies and several different kinds of ice cream. We planned to walk down to the pizza restaurant for dinner and then it would be movies and lots of giggles at our family room camp out.

My husband took the car down to the car wash and I knew that the kids would not be here for a few minutes, so I decided to walk across the street to get our mail from our neighbor Arlene. She had been picking our mail up for us while we were away.

The mail was neatly stacked in a large pile and securely placed in a small open box over on her table. She politely asked if we got everything settled and if they had ever figured out what had caused all of the severe winds storms. I briefly told her that we had found our friends, the storms were over and the town would soon be cleaned up and back together. I thanked her and then I headed home to glance through the mail before all of the grandkids got there.

I placed the bills in a private bin and then I sorted out all of the junk mail, magazines and flyers. I came across a bright yellow envelope that was addressed to me, but it did not have a name or return address on the top. I pulled out the card that was inside of the envelope and it had a colorful bright sunshine on the front that said,

THINKING OF YOU

The inside read,

MAY YOU ALWAYS WALK IN THE 'SONSHINE'

It had been almost a year since my accident in Garden Valley and I hadn't even thought about it for the past several months. But I had to smile because there was a surprising picture enclosed inside of the card. It was a wonderful picture of my friends: Suzanne, Margaret, Bobbi, Connie, Darlene, Terrell, Debby and me. We were all linking arms and peacefully sitting in the dirt, on top of a high mountain ridge watching the raging firestorm before us. The fire was so immense; it looked like the entire eastern end of the United States was on fire.

Apparently, one of the husbands had taken a picture of us as we sat together staring into the mesmerizing fire. The picture was very clear. There was total darkness all around us except for the vast hypnotizing flames that danced across the canyon below.

My heart filled with joy as I realized the picture was taken a year ago on our journey through the darkness, as we traveled towards the light. I smiled as I once again reminded myself, "Everything in this world does not have to make sense."

The card was not signed it just said,

Love you my friend

The doorbell rang and I placed the cherished card and picture up in the cupboard; the grandkids had arrived.

www.ingramcontent.com/pod-product-compliance
Lightning Source LLC
Chambersburg PA
CBHW072234170626
46813CB00003B/1227